Also by Les Pendleton

FICTION

PRIDE AND PRIVILEGE

WIDOW WALK

EVENING

DISINTEGRATION

THE SEA LES TRAVELED

THE SEA'QUEL' LES TRAVELED

NON-FICTION

THE DEVIL, ME AND JERRY LEE

SEA OF GREED

Treasure

LES PENDLETON

Essie Press

Palm Coast Services Inc. dba *Essie Press*
901 Sawgrass Court
New Bern, NC 28560
www.essiepress.com
EMAIL: essie-press@lespendleton.com

This book is a work of fiction. The characters, names, incidents, dialogue and plot are the products of the author's imagination or are used fictitiously. Any resemblance to actual persons or events is purely coincidental. Some of the places in the book are real.

ISBN for Print: 978-0-9823358-5-7
Ebook 978-0-9754740-2-0

Cover by Damonza

Published in the United States of America

February 2015

This book is dedicated to my Admiral, Crew Member and Soulmate, Susanne Harrison Pendleton…
the only *Treasure* I have ever found.

Acknowledgments

Thanks to my editor, Betsy Barbeau, for her patience and endurance.

Thanks to my friends Tom and Karen Joseph, David and Leigh Pfefferkorn, Lou and Helen Schroder, Jim Fortuna, Joe Thurber, Ed Browning, Kevin Guilfoyle, Ted Clark, Marshall and Collin.

Prologue

Lately, I'd been spending a lot more time at work thinking about the things I wanted to be doing with my life instead of all the things I was supposed to be doing. At fifty-seven, it was beginning to feel like all those "want to do" things were never going to happen. My supervisor had taken notice of my mental absence.

"Jim, what are you working on right now?"

"I'm sorry, Frank. What's the question?"

"I wanted to know what you're doing? I haven't seen much coming from your desk the last couple of months and you know, production is the focus of our operation. It's how we stay ahead of our competition."

"I understand. To tell you the truth, I haven't been as productive as I probably should have been. I'm having some trouble staying focused. I've been thinking a lot lately about life in general. There's so much I was hoping would happen. It just hasn't. Do you ever get the feeling that all the things you hoped for in your life have just gone out the window? That's where I'm at right now."

"Everyone does, Jim. But it's my job to keep everyone moving forward with what we're being paid to do and that's why I'm standing here. Why don't you take some time off and try to get some focus? It's hard to get much work done when your mind is on a field trip. You've been with us a long time, so it won't be a problem. There's only two more days left in the work week, so finish up what you're working on and take a couple of weeks off starting Monday."

"I can't do that, Frank. I really need to be working and save any vacation days for the summer."

"I'm not asking, Jim. You need to figure out what you really want to do before somebody above me starts asking questions. Monday."

"Yes, sir."

After work, I stopped in a small bar I remembered from an office party several years earlier. I never had been a drinker. Occasionally, I'd have a beer with a friend at the house, but the idea of going to a bar for a drink was very foreign to me. It was only 6:00 p.m. and I was normally at home by that time. The place was practically deserted. I ordered a draft and sat at the bar thinking over Frank's comments earlier. It wasn't long before I started thinking about my friend Lou Schroder. The dramatic events that occurred on the last day of his life were still vivid in my memory.

Ethel and Joe Morgan had been on their long–anticipated dream trip to the Outer Banks of North Carolina to celebrate their fiftieth anniversary and were just leaving Ocracoke, a remote island. The only way to get there was to ride one of the ferries operated by the State. From the mainland, it was a long trip, over two hours from Cedar Island or Swan Quarter. The shortest distance was from Hatteras Island, just north of Ocracoke, a forty-minute voyage. The boat was full for the last trip of the day. They were both enjoying the warm lounge upstairs and all of the people-watching it allowed them to do. Ethel was particularly struck by the young couple several seats from them who were quite obviously in love. She started up a conversation with them.

"Where are you folks from?"

"Pittsburgh, Pennsylvania. We're here on our honeymoon. I'm Jeff and this is Alexis." The couple looked at one another and shared the exuberant smile of newlyweds.

"That's just wonderful. I'm so happy for you. How did you like Ocracoke?"

"It was beautiful. We hated to leave, but we've been here for a full week and we have to be back at work on Monday. You know, the real world calls. What about you?"

"I'm Ethel and this is my husband Joe. We're here to celebrate our anniversary. It's been fifty years since we tied the knot."

"Wow. I sure hope we can celebrate our fiftieth anniversary one day. That is so special."

"I'm sure you will. We had wanted to visit Ocracoke for years. This just seemed like the perfect opportunity. My, it certainly seems to be blowing hard outside," said Ethel as she turned and looked out the lounge window at the hard rain that was spattering on the glass almost like hail.

"I know. The men at the ferry dock said we were lucky to be on this load, because if the wind had blown any harder, they would have shut the ferry down and we'd be stuck on the island another night. Of course, that wouldn't be too bad, but we would be late getting back to work. Jeff starts his new job Monday, and it wouldn't be good to be late the first week. Goodness, did you feel that gust of wind hit the boat? I think we'll step outside for just a minute and check the weather."

The young couple left the salon for the open deck just outside. It was two stories above the car deck below. Several other passengers were on the outside observatory deck marveling at the extreme weather the ferry was in. Even that high in the air, the wind-driven salt spray stung their faces. There was a distinct feeling of concern aboard. It was a terrible night with winds well over gale force and waves pounding hard against the ferry's bow. As the waves smashed into the steel hull, the large car-carrying vessel shuddered before muscling through, causing a huge cloud of cold, salty spray to fall on all those aboard and their cars. Passengers continued to move about on the ship. It would have been hard to miss the lugubrious looks on their faces or to overhear their comments about the deteriorating weather. Surely, the North Carolina Department of Transportation would never let these vessels operate when the conditions were too dangerous. There was a professional crew and an experienced captain at the helm and, while it was an unnerving ride, it was nothing to be worried about.

Suddenly, the large ferry began to turn wildly in the narrow channel. No one knew what was happening. In moments, the ferry's hull bucked wildly like a mustang at a rodeo trying to shake off its rider. The uniform rhythm of waves breaking against the bow was gone; they now came from every direction, washing over the flat metal deck, hitting the cars and trucks. A van slipped past the chocks holding it in place, slamming into the car in front of it. The occupants in the car immediately jumped out, only to be swept overboard by the next wave. Their screams could barely be heard over the roar of wind and water.

Pandemonium filled the freezing night air as the passengers realized the boat was out of control. Wind, waves, and rapid currents pushed the flat-bottomed ship toward the monstrous breakers waiting just outside the narrow channel. As the drifting boat hit the churning ocean in the inlet, every vehicle on it became a two-ton projectile. The screams of passengers – men, women, and children – could now be heard even above the howling wind and the crashing seas as they were crushed between vehicles or washed over the side of the ferry into the frigid waters. The hull of the ferry struck the hard, shallow bottom in the ocean surf to the side of the inlet. Twenty-foot tall breakers lifted the ship up and down like a child picking up a toy. In moments, all of the vehicles had been dumped into the raging surf. The ferry continued bouncing off the bottom of the ocean floor until its welded seams along the entire length of its hull broke apart. Water filled the hull, the vessel quickly sank, and the lights went dark. The honeymooning couple now hugged each other tightly as they clung to the railing on the top deck. When the ship rolled, they both fell into the frigid, black water, and within seconds, their new life together had ended.

No more screams could be heard. The sea had taken the ship, its crew, and all the passengers. The waters off Cape Hatteras claimed more victims to join the thousands of others lying beneath its cobalt surface. Another group of headstones could be added to the Graveyard of the Atlantic.

* * *

I played this ferry disaster over in my mind as I had many times before. I knew that tragedy hadn't happened. However, it came closer to being a reality than most people ever knew. What actually occurred could easily have had that outcome were it not for the extraordinary set of actual events that unfolded that fateful September night. Hatteras Inlet is one of the most treacherous bodies of water on the planet. Emptying into what has deservedly become known as the Graveyard of the Atlantic, it consists of massive shoals extending many miles into the ocean. No sooner do the shoals end, than the swift movement of the Gulf Stream takes over, adding horrendous currents and unstable weather patterns to the mix. This creates a dangerous froth of rough seas and shallow waters that are more than a match for any vessel unfortunate enough to venture there when Mother Nature is in a foul mood.

The evening of September 19, 2008, proved to be one of those times for the *Cape Point*, a one-hundred-fifty foot ferry plying the waters of the Intracoastal Waterway just inside of Hatteras Inlet. Aboard her were close to sixty passengers and twenty-six vehicles making the forty-five minute trip between Ocracoke Island and Hatteras Village. My great friend, Captain Lowell Schroder, known to us simply as Lou, stood at the wheel.

He was a large, gregarious man with a head full of white hair and a great smile. He had been handling boats for many years. It was his passion.

Lou made his fortune early in life as an inventor of several tools used in his machine shop, and he had used the money to follow his dream. At forty-two years of age, he retired from the machine shop and bought a sailboat. Over the next twenty-odd years, he sailed her everywhere the wind blew, anywhere he had an itch to see.

Eventually, Lou moved to New Bern, North Carolina, with his wife, Helen and son, Chris. He took a seasonal job as a ferry captain with the North Carolina Division of Ferries.

Captains and crew worked seven, twelve-hour days, and then had seven days off. In addition to working the grueling schedule, Lou's health had not been good for a number of years. He was unhappy with the side effects of prescription drugs he was taking. He decided that he could control these health problems through diet and exercise, so he quit taking his pills "cold turkey." It was this unfortunate decision that one week later brought about the horrendous events on the bitter, cold, and stormy evening of September 19, 2008.

* * *

Lou always described the short trip between the two islands on the Outer Banks as "treacherous and nerve racking." The water inside the inlet was extremely shallow and constantly shoaling. Every week, one or more of the ferries would run aground during the trip and have to be pulled off the sand bars by another of the ferries running the reverse trip on the same route. The waters just inside the inlet could get very rough when the weather kicked up. The combination of large waves over shallow water meant the captains had to use extreme concentration and all their skills to make the trip seem routine to the passengers onboard.

On this particular evening, the weather was deteriorating. The wind was approaching forty knots and blowing straight out the inlet toward the ocean. A forty-knot wind outside of Hatteras Inlet would produce conditions that could only be described as violent. Despite departmental rules that dictated the ferries stop running if the wind reached forty-five knots, Lou and the crew decided that, because this was the last run of the day and the ferry needed to get back to where it had originated, the trip would be made despite the risk.

In addition to the treacherous winds, the tide was going out, and the combination of the wind and water running out the inlet meant there would be a lot of forces working against the ferry's trip home. The top-heavy configuration of the ferry made it a perfect target for the high winds and keeping her on course became very difficult.

It was around nine in the evening, and Lou was glad this was his last run for the day. He was tired and not feeling well, and had to fight the wheel to keep *Cape Point* in the middle of the channel. He had just crossed the intersection of the Intracoastal Waterway and the waters flowing out toward the dangerous inlet. It was much more stressful than usual. Lou strained to see the markers ahead and to hold his course when, with no forewarning, Lou's chest exploded into a crescendo of pain and tightness. In less than five seconds, he collapsed onto the ship's wheel, falling forward onto the instrument panel, striking his head. The instrument panel and the counter holding it did nothing to prevent him from falling out of his seat and onto the floor. He was dead before his large frame touched the steel decking. While Lou's pain and worries were over, the mayhem for the remaining crew and passengers was just about to begin.

A crewmember, having noticed the ferry was slowly veering off course, climbed the outside stairs to the wheelhouse to see what was going on and was stunned to see Lou lying on the floor. He immediately ran over to him and, finding the captain unconscious with blood under his head, pushed the ship's engine back into neutral. A major concern slapped the crewman in the face, as he didn't know how to operate the vessel and neither did any of the other crew members on the boat. They were simply there to handle the lines and load and unload the vehicles. The only other crewman able to operate the ferry had just gotten off at Ocracoke to spend the night with his family.

Crewmembers, at a loss for what to do, approached passengers in the lounge and on the deck, asking if there were any boat captains among them. Chaos ensued. With no positive results, they began rapping on windows asking the same question to passengers still in their vehicles, which is where they found Jason Bosley, on vacation from Mississippi. Despite being only thirty-five years of age, he had been a boat pilot for many years. He rushed to the bridge and saw two other passengers, both nurses, trying to revive the downed captain to no avail. Jason didn't know where the boat was in relationship to its normal course, but he did know how the controls worked. There were lighted channel markers that any good skipper could use to determine where the channel was, so he worked to stabilize the vessel and keep her in the middle of the channel. He could see another ferry approaching from the other direction, so he used the ship's radio to contact it.

In a stroke of good luck, the passing ferry had a second, off-duty captain on board. With what had to be a very dangerous and risky maneuver, the two boats were brought tightly together in the middle of the rough sea conditions. The captain jumped from his vessel to the *Cape Point*. Once aboard, he was able to pilot the *Cape Point* safely on to Hatteras Island.

There was no doubt that Jason Bosley saved many lives that night. If the ferry had remained adrift without an operator, it would have been swept out through Hatteras Inlet, and would certainly have been lost with all aboard. A huge disaster had been averted by the swift actions of a passenger. It was truly a miracle.

The State downplayed the event with only a small mention in the North Carolina newspapers. For the most part, they said that no one was ever in danger, but everyone aboard the ferry had a very different view of the event.

An ambulance was waiting for the ferry as it docked, and Lou was taken to the hospital where it was determined he had died instantly from a massive heart attack. Lou's memorial service was held on his sixty-fifth birthday. The huge turnout proved that he had been well loved in the community of New Bern where he lived. It was hard for everyone who attended, as he had been a good friend to a lot of people. The ceremony went on for well over an hour, and perhaps the most difficult part was hearing a translator speak for his profoundly deaf son Chris as he told how good Lou had been to him, and how much he loved his dad. Everyone was completely sapped by the emotion of the moment and they were still drying tears from their eyes as the service drew to a close. The program showed that all the planned items had been fulfilled. That would have been fine for the guests in the room, but there was one last event not written in the program. A loud clicking began in the back of the chapel and everyone turned to see the United States Air Force color guard silently march to the front of the room. They removed the flag, which lay draped over Lou's casket, folded it precisely and handed it to his widow, Helen. By this time, no one had any tears left in them. Lou's friends left quickly, heading to a wake at the sailing club where Lou had been a member for many years. As the extremely trying day came to an end, the collection of friends shared memories of Lou's life and drank more than one beer.

Lou's passing was particularly difficult for me. He had been my best friend for over twenty years, and we had spent almost every weekend together, sailing, working on boats, and enjoying his famous home-brewed beer. He was three years older than me and knew more about boats than anyone I'd ever met. Boats were my passion as well. I'd loved sailboats since I was a young boy growing up on the James River in Tidewater, Virginia, but I'd never been smart enough to invent anything that would free me from my worldly obligations and leave me spare time to go cruising.

I was going through a divorce when we had first met, so I never had money. I envied Lou for the adventures he'd experienced, and we'd often talk about future trips we'd take together, after I found a way to break free. I never did get to the position where I could take off and simply go sailing.

We'd done a number of short trips together, like the time we brought his forty-foot sloop *Zephyr,* to Beaufort, North Carolina, from Florida. We had some great adventures that only whetted my appetite for more of the same. Lou's death had been a wake-up call for me.

Any plans we had of taking off together died with him. I had come to grips with that fact, but I was not happy about it. I hated every moment of my life from Monday through Friday. My divorce basically bankrupted me, and I still had to think about making money for my children's college educations. I didn't want to die at work staring at some Godforsaken computer screen wishing I was anywhere else, but I would do what I felt an obligation to do for my children. Only then would I be free to try and salvage a few of my dreams before heading into that great ethereal sea in the hereafter. This was my fantasy, and it ate at my brain every moment of every day, even filling my dreams at night. I could hear Lou telling me, "Don't wait any longer. You don't know how long you have."

Over the next several years, I continued working and remained depressed about my landlocked situation, but I kept Lou's words in my mind. I paid for my beer and left the bar. I didn't know what I'd do with myself for the next two weeks, but I realized that Frank was right. I needed a break in the worst way. I actually needed a lot more that a break. I needed a severe course correction in my life.

1

To say my own adventure started out innocently enough would be a huge understatement. With winter well underway in North Carolina, I took the opportunity to call several friends and together we came up with the wild idea of driving down to the bluer and warmer waters of the Florida coast, where we could do a little sailing. If there was to be any better place to get my head together, I didn't know where it would be. All of us were experienced sailors with small boats we used mainly on weekends for short jaunts. Occasionally, we took longer trips around the Pamlico Sound or other local waters. However, it never felt satisfying, and certainly didn't fulfill our promises to ourselves of one day sailing off to distant shores on a grand adventure. Like most people who loved the feel of salt spray on their faces and wind in their hair, we all dreamed of "the big one," a trip to distant islands, crossing oceans, sailing into the sunset on the greatest of escapes.

It was certainly never far from my train of thought. We all agreed this would be the perfect opportunity, so we decided to drive to Florida where we would charter a sailboat for a couple of weeks and sail to the Bahamas.

Plans for the trip started to firm up the first night out, while we were all seated on stools at the Buccaneer Bar in Marathon, Florida. None of us were wealthy or retired, but we all shared that same dream of sailing off to an adventure at some point in our lives, and we knew the likelihood of this actually coming to pass was as small for us as it was for anyone else. With a mortgage, a bad economy, kids to send to college, and aging parents to take care of, it was an even more distant possibility for me. However, on that fall night, with a beautiful sunset dropping into the ocean behind the ramshackle bar, a great reggae tune coming from the joint's speakers, and my best friends sharing the moment with me, I really didn't give a crap about anything else. Even my boss Frank had faded from my mind. There were palm trees just outside on the patio, the temperature was perfect, and I had enough money to buy all the beer and chips I wanted. I could pretend I was anywhere for one evening.

I didn't have the slightest clue that this would be the night that would forever change my life.

"A toast."

Tom, David, Tuna, and I all raised our beer mugs.

"Here's to Lou Schroder, a great sailor, adventurer, friend. Lou, without you we'd all be back home at work. Here's to you, buddy. To Lou."

We all took a swig from our glasses and settled back to enjoy the moment and our surroundings. The Buccaneer Bar wasn't like most marina bars that are nestled in small coves near every port on the coast of Florida. It didn't have the jazzy lighted sign by the highway or a paved parking lot with painted lines. In fact, it didn't even have air conditioning or real walls to speak of. It was basically a thatched roofed lean-to that was lucky to not have been condemned. It did have a half dozen rusted out ceiling fans that generated enough air to stay reasonably cool on those rare days when the Gulf of Mexico didn't supply enough wind to handle the task. The sheer unpretentiousness of the place played a large part of what made it special to us. There was the small neon sign reading OPEN and a couple others plugging different brands of beer. I had always been partial to Corona signs. They had a lighted palm tree on them, and I could easily imagine myself lying back on the deck of a sailboat, near some remote beach, Corona in hand.

Tom, Jim, Tuna and David

The emphasis was not so much on what the Buccaneer looked like as it was on the characters that sat on the vintage bamboo and wicker barstools. It didn't take more than one glance around the place to know there were enough stories in that room to fill the entire Library of Congress. One thing was certain about the patrons; you wouldn't find any of them wearing a blue blazer with an embroidered gold yachting emblem on it. Most captains and owners of "gold-platers," the nautical slang for multi-million dollar yachts, would not be caught dead in a place like this. That was just another point in the Buccaneer Bar's favor to my way of thinking. Even if I had inherited office buildings in Manhattan and had money running out my pores, I would never have considered buying a boat I couldn't handle by myself.

You could always tell the difference between weekend cruisers and those unique creatures we all knew as *live-aboards*. They didn't portray the kind of lifestyle that I envisioned when dreaming about going cruising. However, they were doing what we wished we could do, even though they were doing it on the cheap. The extreme cheap. They were almost always men, universally unattached. If you didn't know they were living on sailboats, you would probably mistake them for panhandlers or street people. Their uniforms were shabby clothing permeated with the smell of sweat, salt, and diesel fuel, and most of them needed to double up on their bathing routines. God forbid they consider shaving. Their boats were generally as unkempt as they were, and I doubt many of them had moved from their anchorages for many years. They were basically hermits on the water; men trying to escape the reality of a hard, cold world by living in a small peapod, which had become their own island. It was as if they were attempting to be somewhere light-years away from all the things they no longer wanted to be a part of.

One of these unique individuals had been sitting at the end of the bar listening to our wishful conversations, quietly studying us. In between sizing us up and sipping his rum, he would turn his head toward the quiet anchorage, seeming to see things none of the rest of us could see. During a lull in our conversations, he turned and looked me square in the eye, produced a worn corncob pipe and lighter from nowhere, and lit the thing while sitting almost directly under the No Smoking sign. He was in need of a haircut, a shave, and probably a bath, but I didn't want to get close enough to make that determination. He was a smallish sort of guy, maybe five feet eight at the most, thin and worn looking. It was hard to tell just how old he might have been; a hard life on the water under an unrelenting sun can really age a person. It was easy to see he had a lot of miles under his keel.

"So, you think you'd get some kind of thrill out of sailing the seven seas, do you? Let me tell you one thing, my friend. The sea, the real sea, is a whole lot bigger than most folks think. You know the world is about seventy percent ocean, don't you?"

"Well, I've heard some figure. I'm not sure exactly."

"Take my word for it; seventy percent is right on target. You can get on a boat; even a ninety-footer like mine, and it feels real small out there. Sometimes you feel you ain't doing much more than just hanging on to a piece of driftwood for dear life. Yep. It can get real interesting."

He knew he had piqued my interest so he paused, took a deep draw from his old pipe, and sort of half winked as he looked at me. I held out my hand to him. "I'm Jim Hardison, from North Carolina. What did you say your name was?"

"Didn't say. But since you asked, my name is William Bowen, but folks round here think it's kinda fun to call me Bones, after that old character in the book. You know the pirate book."

"Oh, Billy Bones, like in *Treasure Island*?"

"That's it. Sort of silly, but some folks get a kick out of it, what with me living on an old boat and all."

"You say your boat is ninety feet long?"

"That right. She's an old Alden schooner. She's actually eighty-four foot long."

"That's got to be similar to the Alden they used to film *Adventures in Paradise* back in the 60s."

"You surprise me, Jim. You know a little something about boats. She's a sister ship to *Pilgrim's Progress*. That's the real name of the *Leaky Tiki* you're talking about."

"That's incredible. Where do you keep her?"

"'Bout a mile or two from here. She's at anchor in a little cove. Can't afford no slip in a marina. They charge by the foot and I'm sort of strapped for cash right now, trying to keep bottom paint on the old girl and still make it on a little pension."

"I understand that. I have a small sloop back at home, and after my divorce, I've been lucky to just hang on to her."

"Yeah, divorce can be as nasty as a gale at sea. And it pains you a hell of a lot longer."

"An Alden schooner. That's the kind of boat that fuels a sailor's fantasies. I'd love to see her."

"You in a car?"

"Yes. How come?"

"You throw my bike in the back and drive me to the boat, and I'll not only give you the grand tour, but we can sip a little brandy I keep in the aft locker. What do you say, Jim Hawkins?"

"Jim Hardison. Not Hawkins."

"I'm just messing with you. You remember who Jim Hawkins was, don't you, friend?"

"Sounds familiar. Who is he?"

"The pirate book you was talking about, "Treasure Island" by Robert Louis Stevenson. Just about the best book ever written, at least if you're a sailor."

"That's right. I remember now. He was the kid that befriended the old pirate, Long John Silver."

"You got it. So, Jim, you driving me home?"

"Do you mind if a couple of friends come along? It's actually my buddy Tom's car."

"The more the merrier, as they say. Damn, I forgot my wallet. Don't suppose you could catch my tab do you? I'll get it back to you at the boat."

I should have seen that one coming. I don't know why I thought some strange guy who had ridden his bicycle to a bar and couldn't pay his bill would have anything we would be envious of but, for some reason, I sensed there was more to Bones than was visible on his crusty exterior. I turned to the guys and explained what was happening, and they jumped at the chance to go see an old Alden schooner.

As we stood up to leave, I watched Bones struggle to get off his stool. It was obvious that he had a bum leg. He saw me watching and offered an explanation without my asking, pulling up his left pant leg about six inches to reveal a prosthetic device and rapping upon it below the knee, causing a wooden echo. "Vietnam. Lost it to a grenade. I'm used to it now, but to say the least, it sure limits what I can do on my old boat. On the other hand, it did get me a pension that lets me hang out in the Buccaneer and meet nice folks like you guys. How 'bout giving me a hand throwing my bike in your trunk?"

Tom, walking along with us, easily lifted the bike up onto the roof of his rented SUV and secured it with a couple of bungee cords. The five of us piled into the car and started down the road with Bones serving as our navigator.

Despite being an audiologist out of New Bern and a die-hard sailor, if any one of us could be considered a jock, it was Tom. Though he was in his late fifties, he was very fit, athletic, and six inches taller than any of the rest of us. He never missed a football game if his alma mater, East Carolina University, was playing, and he was a fun loving guy who could put a beer away with the best of us.

Tom

Along for the ride too was David Pfefferkorn, a retired yacht broker who not only looked like Santa Claus, but had an equally jovial personality. He was a talented musician who could play a number of instruments and loved to entertain friends with tunes from the '60s in his musical prime.

David

Then there was our resident super geek, Jim Fortuna. With two of us named Jim, he was assigned the nickname Tuna. It played off his name and had a nautical ring to it, so it stuck.

Tuna

We all shared one thing other than being in love with boats: we were all divorced. All except David who was separated. We were more than a little bitter about our experiences, and David was two years into his separation from his wife of twenty-three years. He had twin boys he loved dearly, but he and his wife couldn't seem to agree on anything except the realization they wanted to be away from each other. Having been a yacht broker for many years, he had one observation he always stressed, and that was the one common ingredient fueling most transactions involving boats: marital status. The mantra goes, "Get divorced, buy a boat. Get married, sell the boat." He was now living proof.

I knew there were many exceptions to the saying but the truth from my perspective was that most women just didn't get the same enjoyment from sailing that men did. The remarks I'd heard from women were that sailboats are slow, small, and a lot of work; at least that's what I'd heard countless times from my wife before our divorce. However, I was without her but still had my little boat, a thirty foot, full-keel sloop – an old Pearson. It was my escape into heaven whenever I got down in the dumps or things weren't going well in my life. When I was on my old sloop, all was right with my world.

As we drove down the pothole strewn road, I looked back at the sleepy, little bar. It was early evening and the sun was just barely down. A small amount of light shadowed the palm trees around the open-air room, and the light of the blue neon beer signs cast a beautiful glow on the interior. Even though this night was a just a small version of my continual fantasies of sailing off to distant islands, having adventures, and living where there were hundreds of palm trees and ladies in skimpy bikinis, it sure beat the heck out of a lot of places north of here.

2

We started down the narrow, two-lane road to the cove where Bones told us his boat lay at anchor. To tell the truth, we weren't expecting very much. Most of the boats these old hermits lived aboard were barely afloat, and the cities where they were staying considered them an eyesore for the tourists whose dollars they relied on for survival. Bones directed Tom down a small dirt road that was more of a path than a road; there were no houses or lights. I was probably not the only one in the car starting to get a little nervous about where he was taking us. After about a tenth of a mile, he told Tom to pull over to a grassy area and park the car. We'd walk the rest of the way. I kept looking in the tall grass for alligators and snakes. I didn't like walking in tall weeds where I couldn't see the ground, especially in the dark.

"I have to keep her down here where they don't charge me nothing. Not a lot of places around here that's deep enough to berth a full keel schooner the size of *Dark Lady*."

"That's her name? Where does that come from?"

"She's a lady and her hull is dark blue. Always liked the looks of a dark hull with fair lines. You can judge for yourself. Here she is."

It was a dark night, but the moon was just starting to get high enough in the sky to offer a little illumination on the water. Directly in front of us was the shadowy outline of a large vessel resting comfortably at anchor about twenty-five yards offshore.

"There she is, boys. A fairer vessel never plied these here parts. She's strong, fast, and lovely. The only lady I ever wanted. I've got a little dory pulled up in the bushes over here. It's going to take two trips to get all of us out there. Who's gonna row the boat?"

"You don't have a motor on the dinghy?"

"I've got one for it out on the big boat. Just don't like the noise. Hell, if you can't row a hundred feet, why in God's name would you want a sailboat? Sailboats ain't nothing but work. You have to be fit to sail one. Sailboats don't like weak men. You know the old saying, don't you?"

"Which one?"

"Wooden ships and iron men. That's how the whole dang planet got discovered. No place on the sea for sissies. So, I row my boat. Does get kinda cold out here in January, but it makes me appreciate a warm shot of brandy and my bunk."

I knew he was right. I volunteered, "I'll get the first three of us out and I guess Tom can row back to pick up Tuna. Let's get this dinghy pushed out here a little."

Bones reminded us of where we were, "Careful for the 'gators, there's plenty of 'em around here."

That got everyone stepping higher. Within a few minutes, we were alongside *Dark Lady*. As we approached, I could see a small soft light through a salon port. The first impression I had of her was that she was large, very large, and traditional looking. It would be easy to visualize her at anchor in Gloucester Harbor a hundred years earlier. Her lines were beautiful, easily what Bones had said she was, an Alden.

John Alden had been a turn-of-the-century naval architect whose drafting board produced some of the most famous vessels of his time. These sailing craft were sleek, narrow, and fast, made by the best boatyards. Quite a few were still around, a testament to the strength of their construction and quality of their design. I had never seen one close up, and I was ecstatic to have the chance to explore the inner recesses of one. David and I helped Bones aboard, while Tom turned the dinghy around to go fetch Tuna. As I stepped aboard, the unmistakable smell of wood and canvas permeated my head and imagination. This was the kind of ship I'd dreamed of since my childhood. I rubbed my hands on the varnished cap rail that topped off the sides of the boat from bow to stern. It was smooth and freshly varnished. Dark Lady was obviously well maintained.

"Bones, this is a floating museum. Do you mind if I walk around the deck a little?"

"Help yourself. She loves to be admired. I'll go below to see if I can find a little of the devil's brew to share with you fellas."

Even though it was dark, I could tell that *Dark Lady* was orderly. Lines were properly stowed on their belaying pins and nothing was out of place topside. The decks were uncluttered and showed an incredible amount of teak stretching her entire length. To replace that today would cost enough to buy a new Ferrari. I walked from bow to stern taking in every detail I could make out in the dim light. I would have loved to have seen her in the daylight and, even better, I would have given a week's pay to sail on her. I looked out through the ratlines that created the rope steps leading up the rigging to the mast. On shore, I could see the lights of homes, and in the distance I could hear a steel drum melody coming from another of the many bars. My fantasy spell was interrupted by the noise of the dinghy coming alongside with Tuna and Tom.

"Guys, you aren't going to believe this boat."

Bones came topside and stood by the side rail as the three of us repeated the tour I had just taken. It would be a tremendous understatement to say everyone was in awe of this beautiful old schooner. We circled the deck several times, savoring the experience. None of us had ever had the opportunity to touch a craft of this nature.

"You boys ready to go below? I've got a light going in the salon and bottle of the best brandy you ever dipped a tooth in."

"Lead on, Bones."

As he took the lead, his profound limp became more obvious. He never complained and seemed to be able to navigate the topsides of his ship with little difficulty despite his handicap.

If we thought the topside of *Dark Lady* was incredible, we were in for an even bigger surprise below. The woodwork was superlative in every way. The cabinetry and bright work spoke of a bygone era when there was extreme craftsmanship and pride put into every board. The one thing I kept pondering was how on earth Bones could keep a boat like this in this kind of condition. It would be a lot of work for a crew of five, and would take at least that many crew to sail her. This was not a boat loaded with electric winches and power assists for every task. This was a boat that would devour manpower, requiring muscles for almost every job, and on a wooden ship approaching ninety feet, there would be more work to be done than one could imagine. The companionway steps were a work of art. They were handmade of polished mahogany and featured a curve that gave them the appearance of a slightly-spiraled staircase. The furniture in the salon was Victorian and lights adorning the walls were polished brass. Bones grabbed an overstuffed, burgundy leather captain's chair and sat at the head of the polished teak salon table and addressed our biggest question without us having to ask it.

"Well, boys, she's a beauty, ain't she? I'm sure you're all asking yourself how'd an old windbag like me got hold of such a ship as this? It's an interesting story. Tell you what, let's take a little sip of the captain's best here, and I'll tell you all about it."

He took five shot glasses from a beautiful liquor cabinet with a stained glass door and carefully filled each one to the brim with brandy. We each accepted the glasses as Bones offered a very interesting toast:

"Here's to finding a goodly crew
to help ol' Captain Bones
To find his chest
And set his soul to rest
'Fore bending sails to home.
Cheers, mateys!"

We all downed the first shot with more than a couple of coughs in response to the strong spirits. Bones took a long drag from his pipe, refilled his shot glass with brandy and started to enlighten us as to how he had arrived at his present state of existence.

"The *Dark Lady* has been my home for almost thirty years. I didn't own her back then, though. Before I joined the service and lost my leg in 'Nam, I had worked for a while at a boat yard and learned a lot about what they're made of and how to take care of them. It's a labor of love, boys. A pure labor of love. But after I got hurt, there was no way I could work in a boat yard. Sure, they got plenty of guys working in 'em that are missing fingers thanks to a slip on a table saw, but nobody with just one leg.

"I was living back home where I grew up, near Bar Harbor in Maine. Folks are not real good about hiring men who only have one good leg and no good education. 'Bout the only job I could find was as a short order cook. It was pretty damned hard standing up all night long on just one leg, but it was all I could do."

As in the bar, Bones again tapped his prosthetic leg when speaking of it. As he spoke, he took pains to look us each in the eye as if to make certain we were all paying attention. There was no question he had us all more than engaged in his story.

"I lived real cheap and saved every penny I got my hands on, because if there's one thing about Maine that I couldn't take, it's those damned winters that far north which are pure brutal. I knew I wasn't going to survive up there in the cold, so after I'd saved up enough money from the grill, I hitched rides on boats heading south, cooking for my passage.

"I don't enjoy it much, cooking, but in all honesty I could run a first class waffle shop. Breakfast was always my favorite meal of the day and there's nothing quite as good as starting the day with a fresh, black coffee and a plate full of hot bacon and eggs over easy. Hell, I could eat a plate of them right now. *Dark Lady*'s got a first class galley."

As he spoke, he looked back toward the galley. It was glistening with polished countertops and a collection of stainless knives blade down in a butcher block.

"But back to my story. I kept going south. First to Charleston, then to Savannah, and finally down here to the Keys. I spent about a month knocking around here and Key West. I'll tell you what. Key West ain't no place to live if you feel a little pull of the bottle, if you know what I mean. I spent a month's grocery bill on liquor down there in two days. Marathon's a lot quieter. There's a lot of sailors here and not so many temptations, so I came back up here and tried to find a job cooking since that was all I was any good for. It was tough. Nobody was hiring.

"Then one day I was down at the old Faro Blanco marina, just killing time and watching the boats come and go, when I overhear this guy at another table ask the waiter if he knows anybody that might want a job on his boat as the ship's cook. That kinda jumped out at me. I didn't really want another job as a cook, but I was poorer than a church mouse. I'd even been having thoughts about just ending it all. You know, jumping into the water off Western Sambo reef and sinking to the bottom. I knew I was in trouble and working was my only way out. As soon as the waiter left, I moseyed over to the guy's table and introduced myself. He was a real pleasant old guy. Said his name was Hibbs, Nathan Hibbs. He asked could he buy me a beer and I joined him for several and a sandwich. Well, we hit it off real good. It was like we had been best friends for years. He said he owned a big old schooner, the *Dark Lady,* and he needed somebody to cook for him and his crew. Said it didn't pay much, but that I could live on board, eat, and sleep for free, and get to see a lot of great places. To me it sounded like the perfect situation, so I jumped at the chance. Yeah, me and Captain Hibbs saw most of the world together. He had made a fortune up in New York and bailed out on everything. His wife left him and his kids didn't want much to do with him, so he bought this boat and took off. Can't say as I blamed him. I'd had a bad marriage once myself, before I went to 'Nam. Hell, the war was more peaceful than our apartment, and I slept better in the jungle with Charlie hunting me than I did the last six months we was together. Thought for sure she'd kill me in my sleep.

"Anyway, me and Captain Hibbs were like brothers. Other crewmembers came and went, but I stayed. It wasn't too hard for me to do the work on just one leg since I only had to cook for four or five guys, and at sea it was mostly soup and bread. I'd give 'em a nice meal or two when we hit shore, but it was never a lot of time standing on one leg. And did we ever see a lot of beautiful places. I've been to Tahiti, New Zealand, the Med, and most of South and Central America. I got to know the *Dark Lady* like she was the back of my hand.

"Nathan trusted me and I looked out for him as he got older. He was about twenty years older than me and his health wasn't the best. He didn't want to give up living aboard and the only way he could stay was if somebody helped him with all his medicines and stuff. Toward the end, it was right pathetic. His kids never came to see him, not even to say goodbye. Their mother had convinced them that the old man was a tyrant or something and they just ignored him. The last few years of his life, we mostly just had a slip at the marina and sort of pretended like we might be going somewhere soon. Eventually, he was bedridden and I read to him 'most every night. He loved those Patrick O'Brian books about the sea. I'd read a while; we'd both take a couple shots of brandy; and then he'd fall hard asleep. One morning about eight years ago, he just didn't wake up. Passed away real peaceful-like in his sleep. He was a fine person, good as I ever knew. Treated me like a brother. Anyway, I sent word to his worthless ex-wife and the kids about his dying and, believe it or not, they showed up for his funeral. Of course, they was a lot more interested in his will than anything the preacher had to say about him. I wasn't going to even go to the reading, but his lawyer sent word through the dock master at the marina that I was supposed to be there. I got cleaned up right nice and sat in the lawyer's office in a straight back chair by the door. The kids and the old lady had all the nice leather chairs up against the desk so they wouldn't miss out on hearing what he had left them. Well, it was a really interesting meeting. Turned out Nathan left most of his cash to charity. He left the kids ten grand apiece, his grandkids the same, and the old lady he left a piece of his mind, and that was it. He did one thing I never saw coming though. He left the *Dark Lady* to me, and he also left a sizeable chunk of money in a trust fund to be used to keep the old girl in good shape. That's the reason she looks as good as she does. She gets whatever she needs to keep her Bristol. I sees to her myself.

"She's ready to go to sea tomorrow. Only problem is, there's no money available to pay a crew to take her out. I guess Nathan thought I'd be happy to just live out my days in the marina. Hell, I'm only sixty-eight years old, and I don't feel no worse than I did twenty years back. Nothing I'd like more than to cut the dock lines free and head out. If only I could find me some crew that wanted to go with me. Don't have no money to pay them. So, that's my story. Now what's the story with you fellas?"

Tom, Tuna, Dave, and I all looked at each other. There was no question that we were all having the same exact thought, and Tom put it in words, "Guys, this is the opportunity of a lifetime. We can go as crew with Bones on *Dark Lady* instead of chartering a small boat from some company. Hell, I'd much rather take this old girl out."

David chimed in. "I'm in. I've always wanted to see what sailing on an old ship was like. This would be like going back in time a hundred years. What do you say, Tuna?"

"No objection here. We'll have the sail of a lifetime and save five hundred bucks or more…each. What do you think Bones? You show us what we need to do and we'll be your crew? We'll buy the food and drinks, all the brandy you want, and even do the cooking. All you've got to do is be the captain and keep *Dark Lady* moving."

Bones blew a ring of smoke in the air after sucking it in from his pipe, "Boys, I say you'd make a fine crew, and I'd be proud to sail with you. We can take on some fuel and supplies in the morning and head out before noon. Where did you fellas have in mind going? Not that it matters at all to me."

I knew we were all hoping to sail to several islands in the Bahamas, but we had nothing mapped out. If we sailed to some islands with clear water and palm trees, that was good enough for me.

"Bones, how about the Bahamas? What do you think?"

"Not good right now. Winds are out of the east. Bahamas would be right on the nose and crossing the Gulf Stream in a headwind ain't no fun. Done it a hundred times at least. I do have a good idea, though. Any of you fellas ever been to the Dry Tortugas? Fort Jefferson? Some of the prettiest waters you ever saw. There's an old Civil War fort out there and pretty much nothing else. It's about seventy miles out in the Gulf from Key West. It would give you fellas a good shakedown cruise to get used to *Dark Lady,* and then we can pick a place on the map you all think would be a good spot to visit after that."

We picked up our shot glasses and drank a toast to this new and unexpected change of direction. Taking in the prospect of this voyage, we stayed up very late swapping our best tales of sailing, women, and old boats. I really enjoyed this group of guys and even Bones blended well with everyone. This would be the trip we would all tell our grandkids about.

3

By nine the next morning we had checked out of our hotel, loaded our bags aboard *Dark Lady,* and picked out our berths. There is a very unique smell to the interior of a wooden boat. I had always loved the feel and ambiance of wood compared to the modern fiberglass boats, though I knew I'd never want to own one. The maintenance on a wooden vessel is at least triple what's required for a fiberglass or steel boat. Of course, the new boats never had the charm of the older wooden ships. Still, if I had the money I might be tempted.

Bones was smiling from ear to ear as we showed up. He wasted no time in assigning and explaining duties to each of us. "Boys, you gotta understand that even though you're all great sailors, I'm sure five folks is the bare minimum a boat like this can get by on. But we can do it and we will. I'll guide you through what's got to be done. It's all old hat to me. I'll tell you what though, lads, it's an answered prayer to me to have you fellas here helping to get the old girl under sail again."

Bones directed us thorough shakedown check of all the systems, oil levels, filters, and lines. The process consumed several hours before he finally fired up the old diesel engine that provided power to the boat when the sails weren't raised. It sounded smooth and powerful. Bones skillfully put the engine in gear and *Dark Lady* nudged slowly up to where her anchor chain descended into the dark blue water. There was a manual windlass that we used to raise the massive fisherman anchor. Once it was secured to the anchor plate against the hull, Bones gave the engine a little bit of throttle and our trip was under way. The marina where Bones wanted to buy fuel was only a short distance down the waterway.

For our boats, it would have been a huge dock with tons of room on both ends of our hull. With *Dark Lady*, however, we needed every inch of the dock and her bowsprit stuck out at least ten feet beyond the end of the pier. We eased in to the fuel dock to fill up the tank with diesel fuel, and also took on some fresh water. Bones had said we would just be topping off the fuel tank, but that topping took three hundred gallons of fuel and almost a thousand bucks. We bought about four hundred dollars' worth of groceries and, at the final stop, the liquor store, we spent another three hundred. Since we had been expecting to pay at least that amount chartering a boat, we were no worse off.

By noon, we had finished filling the fuel and water tanks, washing down the deck, and performing the instrument check. All of the equipment was operating beautifully thanks to Bones' unwavering determination to keep *Dark Lady* in top condition. The excitement built exponentially as we threw the dock lines back to the attendant at the fuel docks and started out of the channel to begin our two weeks of adventure.

Dark Lady was big, larger than the boats we had been sailing most of our lives, and pulling into a dock and exiting a harbor was a lot more trying with a boat this size than anything we had previously experienced. With that bowsprit extending out fifteen feet from the bow, underestimating the space she needed to maneuver could be a disastrous mistake. Bones was at the wheel, and it was easy to see that he was comfortable there. He understood exactly how she responded to his turns on the ship's wheel.

This was a very shallow area of the Florida coast and even though *Dark Lady* had a shoal draft for her size, she needed a good ten feet of water under her to feel safe. Looking to either side of the darker blue water in the channel, it was easy to see the light blue water where the depth decreased to as little as a foot or so. On top of that, the channel was very skinny and the bottom was made of limestone. Striking it with a wooden hull would be like running a car into a concrete wall at forty miles per hour. Thanks to Bones' skill, we cleared the anchorage quickly and motored out the channel toward the Gulf of Mexico.

After clearing the shoals, Bones called us all to the wheel. "Okay, boys, time to put up some sail. Let's raise the mainsail first. There's no winch to pull the halyards, so get the loose end of the halyard off the belaying pin at the foot of the mast and run it through the block on the starboard deck. It's gonna take three of you to get her pulled up snug. If you're ready, I'll head her into the wind."

Bones spun the wheel and pointed *Dark Lady* directly into the wind.

"Okay, Mateys, on my command, raise the sail."

All four of us grabbed the end of the line and started to heave with even strokes. Since *Dark Lady* was gaff rigged with heavy wooden booms on the top and the bottom of the sail, it was no light work raising it to the top of the mast. I was thinking as we hoisted the mainsail, *This was a schooner and the mainmast was larger on the aft end of the boat, as was the sail that flew off it. It would be quite a bit heavier to raise than the other sails.* Once the mainsail was up and secured, we hoisted two forward jibs and finally the staysail. The boat carried a tremendous amount of sail, perhaps two thousand square feet or more.

The wind was about forty degrees off our starboard and as Bones turned the old girl to capture it, she leaned over ten degrees to port. As she started to heel, the power that was being generated through her rig and hull was awesome. Over sixty tons of mahogany, teak and oak began to move silently through the water. I marveled at the power of the wind to move such an immense vessel. She began to build speed. In less than thirty seconds, she was moving at a steady nine knots like it was nothing, and a ship like this could handle a lot more. She was certainly not a dog. She had power and speed. I looked back at Bones and he was grinning like a puppy with three peters. As I walked back toward him, he drew me into his happiness. "There's nothing quite like this, eh Hawkins?"

I figured I might as well let him call me by that nickname. In the long run, it would be easier than correcting him fifty times a day.

"Yes, Bones. There's a huge difference in how a wooden boat seems to respond to the sea when compared to fiberglass or steel. I'm not sure what it is. Maybe it's just the properties of the wood, but it feels like it loves the sea more than the other types of boats."

"Yeah, Hawkins. This old girl ain't happy unless she's moving out here. And look at the Gulf, dark blue already with a motion like a momma rocking her baby. God, I've missed this. I can't tell you boys how happy it makes me that you all decided to come along with me and give old Bones probably my last trip before turning in my foulies. I ain't gonna worry about that, though. I'm here now and that's what counts. How 'bout going below and bringing old Bones a cold beer?"

"Little early for a beer, isn't it? How about a coffee?"

"Now, Jim Hawkins, I'm the captain of this here ship and when I need a beer, I need a beer. Just run along and do like I ask you. Don't want me to have you keel-hauled, now do you?"

He smiled when he said it, but it almost sounded like it was something he'd done before or would be willing to do. Anyone who ever read the historical accounts of life at sea understood that keel-hauling was the practice of tying lines to each arm and leg of a man and dropping him off the bow of the boat into the water. The crew would then pull the man along the barnacle-encrusted keel and back up on the other end of the boat… If there was anything left of him. It would have been near impossible to hold your breath long enough, and if it looked like you might be able to do that, there was the ever present entourage of sharks hanging around the stern of the ship, waiting for garbage to be thrown overboard. Of course, a tasty morsel of flesh, bloodied up nicely by the keel might just hit the spot.

But Bones was obviously joking, so I went below and got myself a cup of joe and Bones a beer. As I returned from the galley, Bones stared constantly to windward and only occasionally broke his concentration to take a drag from his ever-present pipe. He had added aviator sunglasses and an old, beat up straw cap to his ensemble, and even though he was small in stature, he looked every bit the old Gloucester ship captain. As the wind and waves continued to build, Bones had *Dark Lady* on a course as straight as a train track, and he played the puffs of wind to keep her at maximum speed.

David had an affinity for speed. Throughout his life, he had sailed mostly Lightning daysailers. They were fast, responsive, and lovely to look at. His years of racing had made him very sensitive to the set of the sails and performance. When he was on a sailboat, he was constantly studying the way the sails were set and functioning or tinkering with them. I was never that bothered by being a knot or so slower than what was possible. I was more interested in looking at the water, the waves, and the sunsets. I considered myself a "blender sailor." According to my definition, that is someone who starts to shorten the sails the moment the boat has enough wind in them to make her heel so far that the margarita blender might fall over. If I was thirty minutes slower getting to port than another boat, who cared? For me, getting there was the most important part, not how fast it happened.

Dark Lady didn't care what I thought though. Today she had a bone in her teeth, pushing up a bow wave as she plowed through the waves. She was flying through five-foot seas. For a smaller vessel, that was enough wave action to cause some pounding or rolling, but not for this old girl.

Throughout the afternoon, the wind continued steady at eighteen knots. The waves had remained around five foot and, despite it being a September afternoon, the sun felt hot on our faces. We had each found a spot on deck where we could be on the ready to adjust sails or follow any orders barked out by Captain Bones. In between those times, we were just breathing in the salt-filled air and soaking up the ambiance of where we were and what we were doing.

David had grabbed his old Martin guitar from his cabin and entertained us all with some great old tunes. For the most part, we could sing at least a verse or two of each song – not very well, but the spirit was there. To feel the wind in the sails, the spray blowing gently over the deck, accompanied by a great rendition of "Margaritaville" was special beyond description.

Toward evening, Bones asked for relief from the wheel and David jumped at the opportunity to take control. Bones joined me on the starboard rail and motioned for Tom and Tuna to join us.

He stared out over the rail and pointed toward the faintly visible shoreline behind us.

"Boys, ain't this lovely? I told you the *Dark Lady* would be the sweetest ride you ever took, didn't I? Now, I need to run something past you fellas. As you can see, the wind is still stiff out of the nor-east. That makes sailing to the Bahamas near impossible. The waves in the Gulfstream would also be pretty damned ferocious with any element of wind out of the north. It'll probably turn around in a couple of days but, 'til then, we'd just be punching ourselves in the nose to keep trying to head east."

We were all hoping the next thing Bones said would not be that we needed to turn around and head back to Marathon. After fueling up and stocking *Dark Lady* with supplies, I didn't have enough money left to cover my share if we had to go back to the original plan and rent a boat in the Bahamas.

"Now don't fret none, boys. I have an idea I want to run by you. Might just be this will excite you just as much as racing over to the Bahamas today. As you can see, the wind is not working with us. *Dark Lady* don't go to wind real good and she's slow as molasses under diesel. That leaves us with the question of what to do 'til the wind turns around. I've got an idea I think you'll like. What do you say we take a couple of days, like I suggested last night, and head with the wind out to the Dry Tortugas? I can tell you honestly the water is even prettier than the Bahamas. It's crystal clear and has the most beautiful neon blue tint to it you ever saw. It would be a great sail from here and we can be over there tomorrow evening. What d'ya say?"

I looked over at Tom and Tuna and said, "Fine by me. I've always wanted to see the Tortugas. I've heard they have some of the best diving waters in the world."

They both agreed and the decision was made.

"Wise decision, boys. With this easterly wind, we'll make great time and have a beautiful night sail. Thanks to you fellas for seeing my way on this one. I'll go give Santa Claus a heading and then I'm going to get me a couple of beers and take a little nap. You fellas take turns at the wheel and I'll check on you every now and again."

It seemed like a logical decision at the time. None of us could have possibly known what it would mean in the long run.

The wind moderated a little during the evening and by dark, it was less than ten knots. We were sliding along at four knots, but the direction was good and I, for one, wasn't in any hurry. The moon appeared from behind us and lit the ocean up to the point that a spotlight wasn't even needed for visibility. The stars were positively brilliant with the big dipper, Orion, and even Cassiopeia adding to the show. It was a magical evening. With no motor running, the sound of water running along the hull was the only noise punctuating the quiet, star-dappled night.

The hours rushed by like minutes, and before long it was my turn at the wheel. Unlike the newer and smaller boats I was used to sailing, *Dark Lady* had a huge wooden wheel, reminiscent of those that steered the clipper ships during the golden age of sailing. It was about five feet in diameter with heavily varnished wooden spoke handles so large it was like grabbing hold of a rocking chair's armrest. The weight and strength of the boat could be felt in the wheel, as could the tension it handled while steering the craft. Each time a puff hit the sails, *Dark Lady* would lean slightly and the wheel would grow harder to turn. It was rhythmic, like holding a baton and leading an orchestra. With my hands on the wheel, I got a bearing from the binnacle-mounted compass and then picked a star out in front of us to steer toward.

Handling *Dark Lady* was even more of a rush than I could have imagined. The sheer power generated by her mammoth sails and sleek hull was awe-inspiring. Even though I had the 2:00 a.m. to 4:00 a.m. shift, I was exhilarated. Just before I was about to give up my turn, Bones appeared from below and came over to check on our progress. He offered no advice as he looked at the compass and GPS. He nodded approvingly, moved to the wooden deck seat in front of the doghouse, sat himself down, crossed his legs like an Indian chief, and pulled a harmonica out of his pocket. He played a series of rhythmic sea chanteys and ended with a beautiful rendition of "Amazing Grace."

I offered some modest applause as he finished. I even heard some clapping from down below where David and Tom were supposedly asleep in their bunks. It added a surreal element to an already spectacular night. Just as strangely as he had appeared, Bones stood up, sheathed his harmonica, and headed back down the companionway steps to his cabin in the aft end of *Dark Lady*.

Bones didn't reappear until the sun was well up. I don't think any of us slept a wink that first night out. I wasn't even tired, and Tuna didn't go below the entire night. About sunrise, he went down to the galley and put on a pot of coffee. The four of us gathered around the wheel and discussed our great fortune in meeting Bones and *Dark Lady*. We lifted our coffee mugs in a toast.

"To *Dark Lady*, Bones, and the Tortugas."

Sunrise swiftly turned into midday and by four in the afternoon, we were all straining our eyes to be the first to spot land. About an hour later, Tom saw the color of the water change on the horizon.

"It's just like Bones described it. It looks like blue neon shining from the sea ahead."

In the water directly in front of us were light blue spots so brilliant that it looked almost like spotlights were glowing from beneath the surface. As we closed on the islands, we saw the red and green channel markers appear. Bones came over and took the wheel.

"Mighty shallow channel through here, Hawkins. How 'bout one of you young fellas shinny up the foremast ratlines and look for coral heads? Don't want to scratch our bottom getting in there."

Tom shot up the ratlines and began to keep a forward vigil. Periodically, he'd yell down "Five degrees to port," "Two to starboard," or "Back her down." The channel was long and winding, and after an hour we came into the anchorage behind the National Park Service dock where the ferries brought tourists from Key West several times a day. Seaplanes also flew people in. After landing, they taxied the planes to the beach just beside the NPS's service docks.

The fort itself was huge. Named Fort Jefferson, a popular tourist and cruiser destination, it was the largest masonry structure in the Americas. Because it was located in a hot, dry climate on an island with no fresh water, cisterns had been constructed to collect rainwater and moats were built around the immense structure for sewage disposal. Unfortunately, with no tides in the area, the rank sewage remained in the canal just outside the fort's walls almost constantly. When troops had lived in the fort, it must have been torture to have the constant stench of sewage in the air.

However, the fort was no longer occupied and the water around the Tortugas was truly remarkable. Bones had not exaggerated when describing the water as being better than in the Bahamas. The color was so amazing and inviting that even though none of us had slept the night before, we were all up for a quick snorkel before turning in for the night. We were just about to hop off the side of the boat when Bones offered some advice.

"Boys, hammerheads get really huge around these parts. They chase the tarpon into the lagoon. I don't think I'd go swimming this far out in the anchorage. Take the dinghy and ease on into shore and dive right around the fort. You'll be a lot safer there. I know there's folks that dive out here and you can suit yourselves, but I've seen 'em in here well over ten feet long, and I'm thinking you don't want to be getting in where folks drop their garbage overboard."

We decided to follow Bones' advice and made two trips to shore with the dinghy to get everyone into a shallower area. Bones stayed with the boat and the beer.

We snorkeled just to the side of the federal docks, near a group of old pilings that used to support some sort of pier. The area was completely packed with tropical fish painted every color of the rainbow that moved in unison as they swam around the bottom of the old structure. Just outside of the pilings were the more ominous guests, the barracudas. There were at least a half dozen of them, the largest being nearly five feet long. Just looking at the long rows of razor-sharp teeth protruding from their closed mouths was enough to make our butts pucker. They seemed to be staring at us with every turn. It was a little unnerving, but we managed to stay out of their way and explore the warm, clear water around the beach.

After an hour of the best snorkeling I'd ever done, we piled back into the dinghy and rowed back out to *Dark Lady*. As we arrived, we saw the National Park Ranger vessel alongside our boat and two officers were on deck speaking with Bones. As we boarded, an officer sternly approached to lecture us on the rules of the park. It was clear by his mannerisms that he thought he had a lot of power. Of course, I really wanted to explain to him that the park and his salary was bought and paid for with our U.S. tax dollars, but I fought off the urge. I knew my presence was not intimidating as I was balding, a little overweight, and looked more like an accountant than a seaman. Small-minded people who had a need to impress me with their authority nonetheless incensed me. I would have liked to have told him what he could do with his authority. Instead, we listened to his rant describing the myriad of things that could and could not be done while we were there. It was a pretty depressing display of how far off-base our government had become in just one short lifetime. When I was growing up, we looked at government employees as civil servants and today, it seems we are their servants. But we were on vacation and listening to a blowhard for twenty minutes seemed like a small price to pay for two weeks of adventure.

Bones complained about their visit at least ten times as much as we did. It was even more remarkable that evening when a Cuban fishing boat came into the anchorage, dropped their hook for the night, and proceeded to break every single rule that the officers had spent so much time educating us about. In the end, while it burned our butts, we figured they thought they weren't supposed to be there in the first place so why should they be beholden to our rules? We stewed some more, had a few beers, and collapsed into our bunks for overdue rest.

I woke up around three in the morning and went topside to check out the anchorage. The moon was full and it lit up the entire lagoon, almost as brightly as an overcast day. I saw lights still burning on the Cubans' small fishing trawler and heard Latin music wafting out over the waves. There was also a good deal of laughter, which meant most of them must still be up. I saw one of their crew take a large rubber trash container and dump the entire contents into the anchorage. Earlier in the evening, they had been cleaning their fish and washing the cutting board off into the water as well. This must have been what Bones had warned us about, why it would not be advisable to get in the water out this far. They were basically chumming the water with the blood and fish guts, so I'd be willing to guarantee that there would be sharks in the area.

The breeze was light but cool, and I could pick out the shadows of palm trees swaying on the shore. It was truly a beautiful place. The one thing it lacked was civilization. As much as I loved nature and the thought of deserted tropical islands, I also liked the thought of a little Tiki hut with a bar on a white sandy beach and a reggae band playing steel drum music. Both played a part in my fantasy of sailing away to paradise. Soon we would be able to partake of the attributes on the other side of my fantasy. At least, I assumed we would.

Just as I was about to head back below for a few more hours sleep, David came topside. "Pretty spectacular, isn't it?"

"You can say that again. Makes me wish we could just keep on sailing, see every little island in the world. When you're out here, the everyday problems just don't seem quite so important."

I became obvious I had brought up a subject we would both like to forget, but could never seem to get ahead of. David offered, "Yeah, if my divorce was final, I think I would just keep on going. Of course, I'd have to get a job on a cruise ship 'cause after my old lady and her attorney get through with me, I won't have enough money to go to a movie. I don't know why I didn't see this coming. I could have set a few bucks aside over the last couple of years and been in a lot better shape. I don't even have the money to get myself a lawyer. She's got a good one and I'll have to pay for that one to screw me while I don't even have one to represent me. Something's really wrong with this picture."

"I feel for you, man. I've been there, just a few years ago. I haven't recovered yet and probably won't. By the time I pay her alimony and rent for the dump I live in, there's nothing left. Sometimes I think I'd be better off to just move to Australia or some other country and tell them all to go screw themselves. It's made me a bitter man. But we're here now, in the tropics on an old schooner, so let's just enjoy what we have."

"You're right, Jim. You never know what tomorrow will bring. Maybe we'll win the lottery."

"It's possible. Of course, I don't buy any tickets so I guess that's a long shot for me."

"Probably so. Well, I think I'm finally ready to turn in again. We'll need some sleep if we're heading to the Bahamas tomorrow."

"Let's hope this wind turns around so we can head east."

We both went below to finish the last few hours of the night in our cabins.

The first rays of dawn revealed that the wind not only hadn't changed directions, but it had actually intensified in strength. It would be nearly impossible to head south, wrap around the Keys and then head east to the Bahamas. It meant we'd be motoring almost the entire trip, and Bones had made it clear that *Dark Lady* didn't move well under diesel alone, that she was built to sail and that's what she needed to be doing. Tuna and Tom whipped up some wonderful scrambled eggs, toast, and coffee for breakfast and we discussed the situation over the meal and, as expected, Bones reiterated that he wanted to keep sailing.

"Well, boys, this might not be what you were thinking about doing to start with, but I got an idea you just might find it interesting. You were planning on sailing for two weeks, if I remember right. It's only a three or four day sail across the Gulf to old Mexicana. I know you've heard of Cancun and Cozumel. The whole coast of southern Mexico is tropical with water even prettier than the Bahamas. There's all kinds of little Mexican towns with pretty señoritas serving rum and fruity drinks, if you get my drift. It would be an incredible sail with twenty knots of wind following us on a broad reach. We'd be sailing and making nine knots the whole way. What do you fellas think about that option?"

I was sold immediately. Tom and Tuna had some concerns about what might happen if we got there and the wind didn't let up. We could be stuck there for a while and they were expected back at their businesses in two weeks. I tried to assuage their worries.

"Guys, look. You wanted adventure. This is even greater than what we were originally thinking about. The Bahamas are great, but they are still pretty much barren, windswept coral flats. Mexico is lush with ancient ruins and real towns along the coast. It would be like visiting another world. If you absolutely had to fly home, they have airports there. Sure, it would cost some to buy a last minute ticket, but wouldn't a trip like this be worth it?"

It didn't take much convincing. The plan made sense and we were all anxious to start sailing again. The Tortugas were beautiful, but there was nothing there to look at other than the old fort. Excitement built as we weighed anchor. Bones came up with some new precautions for the crossing.

"Boys, the Gulf don't look real big on a map but, trust me, it ain't like the seventy mile crossing of the Gulfstream to get to the Bahamas. It's open water, a lot of it. It can get real rough out here and we need to secure everything topside and below before we get too far out there. So let's start stowing everything where it won't be rolling around on deck or in the cabins when it starts to get rough. The wind's already pushing twenty knots and that's going to kick up some pretty big swells. We'll start with the inner headsail and the main and see how she moves with those. It's always easier to add sail than to shorten it in a real blow. We'll kinda ease out there 'til we get a feel for what's happening. Okay, let's get moving on those halyards, boys. Raise sail."

This was exhilarating. To see the sails rise up the huge wooden masts and hear them slap as they filled with wind was like playing a part in "Mutiny on the Bounty." *Dark Lady* was a ship, not just a sailboat. We were her crew and she responded to our efforts. It made me wish I had lived a hundred years earlier when these magnificent vessels were the main mode of transportation, filling every harbor around the world. After we had time to consider the facts more, we were all more excited about heading across the Gulf to Mexico than we had been about heading to the Bahamas.

The weather continued to build and by late afternoon, the wind was pushing a steady twenty-five knots. *Dark Lady* took it in stride and had been at hull speed for the past four hours. She was heeled over to about fifteen degrees and the dark blue waters of the Gulf of Mexico seemed to fly under her sides only to come boiling out behind her. We had no way of getting an update on the weather forecast for this area, other than from NOAA, and their reports didn't cover the weather this far out. There was a single sideband radio onboard but Bones said it hadn't worked for years, so he'd disconnected it. The VHF radio only had a range of thirty miles or so and we were way out beyond that distance. Dark clouds began filling in to the south of us and seemed to be heading our way in a hurry. As they approached, we could see bursts of lightning inside their tops. We recognized that we were about to get hit by a series of thunderstorms within the hour, but we didn't worry. Bones was used to both these waters and *Dark Lady*. He barked out the needed precautions to us.

"Let's shorten the main, boys. We'll leave up the headsail and be prepared to take 'em both down if it gets stronger than I'm thinking it's gonna. Can't ever be too sure about storms like this. Might be a big black cotton ball and nothing to worry about, or it can get real nasty in a hurry."

The waves and wind built quickly. The storm picked up in speed and intensity as it approached. Cracks of thunder became frequent and loud. We could feel the electricity in the air around us. The wind moved up the scale quickly to around sixty knots. We lowered the main and jib leaving up only a small stormsail to help *Dark Lady* maintain steerage. Even with such a tiny amount of sail up, we were moving at over seven knots. Wave heights were approaching ten to twelve feet and our bow flew over the top of one wave and then bit into the next, burying itself two thirds of the way up to the bowsprit.

Even with all of this wind, *Dark Lady* stayed on her feet and under control. She was meant to be here and she knew it. After about ten minutes of high winds and lightning, I felt it: The hair on my arms and the back of my neck stood straight up. There was a loud crack and then a hissing as the electrical current flowed out of the rigging of the boat and into the ocean. It had registered a perfect hit on the mast. The VHF antenna, at least what was left of it, fell onto the deck still smoking.

I had been on boats long enough to know that lightning doesn't affect just one thing. If it strikes a vessel, it usually takes all the electronics out with a single blast. The storm passed as quickly as it had come and a check of the ship's instruments revealed the worst. All the electronics were fried. We were all concerned. In our collective experience, this was a bad situation. However, Bones was pretty nonchalant about it all.

"No need to fret, boys. The old manual compass is still fine. All you gotta do out here is just keep heading due west. That's where Mexico is. No way to get lost. Fact is, I've done this trip so many times, I could do it with my eyes closed. We can look at fixin' the electronics when we get there."

Tuna volunteered to lend his unquestionable expertise to the situation. "I'll survey the damage. Usually, when lightning takes out electronics, they're toast. But if they had good fuses, there's a possibility something might have survived."

As we continued our journey, the seas grew calm again.

4

As we continued to sail *Dark Lady* toward Mexico, events were unfolding ahead that we had no way of knowing would impact our immediate future. The opulent and oversized yacht *Diablo* rested twenty miles to sea due east of Veracruz, Mexico. Onboard, the leader of a large and violent drug cartel and his crew of thugs were preparing two of their own to deliver a valuable load of heroin. They would take it up the coast to a waiting crew aboard a would-be sport fishing yacht near South Padre Island, Texas.

The overlord of the cartel was known as El Dorado. He had made hundreds of millions of tax-free dollars through his illegal enterprises over the past decade. There were many others who wanted to be his replacement and beneficiary of the millions he had made in drug money. His ruthless manner and adept skills at maintaining his enterprises and power, however, were unmatched. El Dorado had a gift for violence and he exceled at some of the most basic skills needed in his trade. He not only didn't shy away from the most virulent forms of violence, he relished the opportunity to use them.

He was considered by his contemporaries a wizard at devising methods of circumventing the authorities both in Mexico and in the States. Those he could not fool, he bought off or executed, and he really didn't care which he had to do. His theory for life was that the only way to maintain power was to be feared. There could be no sign of weakness or his enemies would confront him like sharks in a feeding frenzy.

He had recently come up with an ingenious method of shipping his product north along the coast without anyone having a clue it was being done. He had never liked the primitive methods his rivals used, such as tunneling under the border or having mules risk carrying it on their persons. For many years, he had been perfecting the practice of taking stolen cars with United States license plates and crossing the border with drugs hidden in the fuel tanks. He would kill unsuspecting American tourists just to steal their cars. His own men would serve as drivers and were told to just bail out and run if the car came under suspicion. The authorities would then find only an empty car with an American owner who was nowhere to be found and never would be. The drugs would be confiscated by the authorities but, in truth, it was just a drop of water in an ocean of drugs. For each shipment lost, there were five or more that made it through. It was almost foolproof.

Lately, his imagination and desire for using the sea as a roadway had spurred him to come up with a new and even more inventive method. He had contracted with a boat manufacturer in Panama to build him several two-man submarines with cargo room for several hundred pounds of heroin, and the cruising range needed to reach coastal towns in Texas. Once there, a rendezvous point would be established and an American partner would pretend to be on a fishing trip aboard a forty-foot fishing boat of U.S. registry. After dark, the sub would surface and they'd offload the drugs to the fishing yacht. By dawn, the drugs would be ashore and on the way to cities all over the States. Of course, there was the matter of getting the sub up the coast. There were a few wrinkles he was still trying to work out. The two young Mexicans chosen to drive the sub were getting last minute instructions on what would be required of them. As they spoke in Spanish to the fabled El Dorado, they tried to remain positive, all the time knowing they were embarking on an extremely dangerous task.

"So, you feel like you can do this for me?"

"Si, Señor Dorado. No problem. I need the money for my family as does Hector. We will succeed."

"I'm sure you will. Take your seats in the sub and I'll go over a few details with you."

The men raised the clear glass canopy and squeezed into the two small seats, one directly behind the other.

"Now remember, because you will be twenty feet or so under the surface, your GPS cannot get a position until you surface. You must surface every hour so that your GPS can refresh and give you a new bearing to enter into your autopilot.

"I have a watch for each of you to wear to know exactly when to surface. Every hour, an alarm will sound to alert you that it's time to take the sub to the surface. You will only need to remain there for five minutes. You get the position, enter your new heading and dive back under to about twenty feet. If you do this every hour, then you will stay on course even in the dark. Sanchez, put the special watches on our friends here."

El Dorado's henchman took out two very large, expensive and cumbersome looking devices, and fastened them around each man's wrist. Surprisingly, there was a small stainless steel cable attached to each watch. He attached the other end of the short cable to the seat that each man sat in. Sweat poured from their foreheads and their voices showed the strain of the moment. The men locking them in the boat showed no emotion as they followed the chilling orders.

"Why must you cable us in the boat, Señor Dorado? You are not afraid we will run away with your drugs, are you?"

"Not a bit, my friends. They are just for insurance. Let me tell you how they work: Each watch contains just enough C4 explosive to blow you both to a watery grave. Oh, it would be very quick and probably painless, but you would be dead nonetheless. I would take care of your families for you, of course. Your wife especially, Hector. She is very beautiful. I'm sure she could make me a lot of money working at my brothel in Juarez or Tijuana."

"You are a bastard, Dorado!"

Dorado glanced at his diamond encrusted Rolex as he nonchalantly continued. "Be very careful, my friend. You can be replaced very quickly and never get the chance to save your wife or make ten thousand American dollars. With that money, you can get a new start and perhaps find an easier way to make a living. I'm running late for an appointment, so I must be brief. But to explain to you how this will all work, as you already know, your very special watches will tell you each hour to surface. You should be at the rendezvous point in just under twenty hours. You have enough fuel to make that distance with a little to spare. You will want to make sure you do everything very precisely so that you arrive at the right place in that time frame. The gentleman who will meet you and offload my cargo will have the key to remove these watches. If you tamper with them, I assure you, they will go off. And oh yes, if you don't arrive in twenty one hours and have them removed, they will explode all by themselves. Do you have any questions?"

Neither man spoke. The hate for El Dorado was painted on both of their faces. In mere moments they were gone. It was a long and arduous journey. The space inside the sub was tiny and felt as though they were already in a water-bound coffin. They made the trip within the allotted time and their cargo was offloaded. Unfortunately, but to be expected, their contact knew nothing about a key. They nor their craft were ever seen again. Since the profit from a single successful shipment could run into multi-millions of dollars, two lives and a small sub were very small expenditures.

* * *

Susanne and Karen had looked forward to this trip for two years. They had seen a television show about Mexican resorts and were drawn to the beautiful places that dotted the east coast of the country. With the meager income of schoolteachers, they had combined their savings and picked Cozumel as the destination for their road trip down the coast.

"I'll tell you what, Karen, the travel shows sure didn't mention anything about how bad these roads are. I'll probably need a kidney transplant by the time we get there."

"Just think of it as part of the overall experience. If it was just like driving to South Padre Island, you'd never know we left home."

"And look at these pathetic houses people are living in. This a lot more third world than I was expecting, and I wasn't expecting much. We need gas. Does the map show any towns coming up?"

"Okay. Give me a minute and I'll take a look. You know, Susanne, I'm a lot better driver than a navigator. Hang on and I'll see what's up ahead. Looks like there's a place called Tampiquito. I don't think it's very big."

"They've got to have a gas station, wouldn't you think?"

"Of course they will. All these beat up pickup trucks don't run on hay. I can see some buildings up ahead. That must be it. It's getting pretty darned hot. Remind me to ask the guy at the station if they can check the radiator. I know it's got a small leak and I have to add a little water every so often."

They were both relieved when they spotted a small store just ahead with a single pump out front. They pulled into the dirt and gravel parking lot and up to the pump, shutting the old Explorer down. As they stepped out and looked at their vehicle, they saw that it was so covered with dirt and grime that they could barely tell it was Susanne's beloved silver SUV. She had purchased it new and babied it for the past eight years. It still had only fifty-six thousand miles on it. She planned on keeping it another five or six years. On a teacher's salary, an automobile was a huge expense, and this one was paid for. That's one of the things that had made the trip they were on possible: No car payment.

"Karen, see if they've got a bathroom we can use."

Karen entered the small, run-down store. It was reminiscent of old southern general stores that had dotted Highway 17 on the East Coast of the States about fifty years earlier. It had an antique drink box that was accessed by lifting the lid and sliding a drink inside along a steel canal through cold water, which maintained a reasonable chill. As hot as it was, anything below eighty degrees would taste just fine. Karen went to the counter where a young clerk was stacking cigarettes with his back to the counter, though he was able to cast a glance toward her every five or ten seconds. She realized that both she and Susanne would be recognizable as Americans not for only for the license plates on the car, but also for their overall appearance. They were both in their mid-thirties, but had maintained their looks and physiques with countless hours of cycling. When they were home, they spent almost every weekend looking for new back roads to travel on their mountain bikes. Karen was small, redheaded, and vivacious. Susanne was dark-haired – almost Latin looking – so if she was dressed a little more native, she could easily pass for a villager in this region. Her skin was olive, which made her smile even more brilliant. Together, they were a striking pair and drew approving looks from male bystanders just about everywhere they went. They enjoyed the attention and would, more often than not, smile back at their admirers. The young man quit his stocking duties as Karen approached. This gave her the opportunity to try out her feeble Spanish vocabulary.

"¿Hablas inglés?"

"Sí. Yes, ma'am. What can I help you with?"

"Do you have a bathroom we can use?"

"Yes. It's very clean. The owner's wife is very proud of how we keep the ladies' room." The clerk reached under the counter and picked up a key with a six inch long piece of wood connected to it with an electrical tie. It had *Señoritas* hand lettered on it and it looked as though it might have been made when Pancho Via rode through town. The man pointed through the front door. "The bathroom is around back. Just walk around the building and you'll see it."

"Gracias."

"De nada."

As she walked outside, Susanne looked toward her. Karen held the key out in front of her. "Ladies room in the rear, babe."

"Great, I'll join you. I've got to pee like a race horse."

"That's not real ladylike."

"And your point would be?"

They found the door not only unlocked, but half open, and the inside was not nearly as clean as had been alleged by the clerk. If they hadn't needed to use the bathroom quite so badly, they would have undoubtedly tried to hold it until they got to a slightly bigger town with more modern facilities. After wetting a hand towel and wiping off the toilet seat and the rim of the sink, they took turns using the commode before addressing their hair in the mirror, which only had two minor breaks in it.

"God, these people lead a poverty riddled existence. Everything is old and dirty. I don't think I could ever be happy living like this."

"Why do you think millions of them are in the States? They don't want to be here either. I sure hope the resort area we're headed to is as nice as we think it is. This is a hell of a long drive if it's not. I don't want to have to spend two weeks cleaning off the toilet seat every time I have to pee."

"I'm sure it will be fine. Let's get going. I think we've got another eight or nine hours of driving ahead of us before we see our beautiful hotel sitting on a white sandy beach."

"Don't forget the handsome Latino cabana boys. You promised handsome cabana boys. You aren't going back on that promise, are you?"

"They'll be there. Trust me. Don't forget, I've seen all the Ricardo Montalban movies. Granted, they were black and white and made forty years ago, but it clearly showed these places full of hot-blooded young Latino cabana boys."

"Okay, I'm holding you to it."

As they walked back around the store to return the key and pay for their gas, they were both astounded to see that Susanne's car was not where they had left it. They looked in every direction and it was nowhere to be seen. Their stomachs began to knot. They ran into the store where the attendant was walking back to the counter from a back room. He smiled to them and held out his hand to take back the key.

"Thank you, señoritas. Have a beautiful day."

"Where is our car? We filled up and left it right out front just long enough to go to the bathroom!"

"Oh, señoritas. You didn't leave your keys in the ignition, did you?"

"I might have. What difference does that make? If somebody stole it, they stole it. It doesn't matter if I forgot to take the key with me. I had to use the bathroom in a hurry."

"Well, I'm very sorry, but someone has probably removed your vehicle."

"Removed. Removed! What the hell is that supposed to mean? They stole it. You know that's what they did."

By now, the polite young man had a small smile behind his polite countenance, and it was starting to look like a smirk.

"You're in on it, aren't you? You know exactly where our car is, don't you?"

"Señoritas, please don't say things about me like that. You don't know me. I would never steal anything from anyone. It hurts my feelings when you say such things about me."

"Oh, I'm sure. You have a very fragile ego. If that's the way you're going to be, we're going to just call the cops. Do you have a phone we can use?"

"Of course, right here behind the counter. You're welcome to use it. The number for the police is written on the card right beside it. They have an office just down the street. It won't take them long to get here, and they can help you find your car."

As Susanne attempted to dial the number, her worst fear was confirmed when she saw her Texas Rangers baseball cap stuck under the counter. She couldn't contain herself any longer. She was not the kind of woman to back down or play the part of a scared, frail little woman. She went hundred eighty degrees in the other direction.

"You little creep! That's my ball cap. It was on the back seat of my car. You stole it."

"I'm sorry, señoritas, but that's my hat. I've been a Texas Rangers fan for many years and my cousin who lives in Houston, Texas, sent that to me three years ago."

"Is that so? Then how come it has last year's date on the strap? How can you explain that, you sorry little thief?"

"I'm going to have to ask you ladies to leave my store. You have insulted me and called me a thief with no provocation at all. If you don't go, I'll have to call the policía myself."

"Why don't you go ahead and do that? We'll stand right here and wait, unless you think you're big enough to throw me out."

"Okay, señoritas. I'll call them right now."

Susanne and Karen stood beside the front door of the store giving disgusted looks at the young man who smiled the entire next hour until a single, ten-year-old Ford pickup truck with a red light on the top pulled into the parking lot. An overweight, cigarette smoking cop got out and, ignoring them, went straight into the store to see the clerk. They exchanged pleasantries in Spanish, smiling and laughing aloud for about fifteen minutes before the policeman came to speak with the girls.

"Good day, señoritas. I understand you have a complaint of some sort?"

With an exaggerated show of hands in the air and ever-increasing pissed off tone to her voice, Susanne vented to the officer. "It's not a complaint. It's a report. Our car was stolen right here in front of the store while we were in the bathroom."

"I see. The clerk told me that you left your keys in the ignition. In this very poor part of the world that is almost an invitation of sorts to some folks. We are not rich like people in the United States. We are a very poor people."

"What you're saying is, if I have a nice car and some poor person down here doesn't, it's just fine to steal my car?"

"Of course not. Stealing is never acceptable. I'm just saying that it's understandable how something like this might happen. I'm sure that someone must have had some sort of emergency and perhaps no way to get to the hospital, maybe with a child or loved one. They saw your lovely silver car sitting there with the keys in it and just borrowed it. I'm sure they'll pull it over to the side of the road when they are done with it in a couple of days or so, and you'll have it back no worse for wear. You are worrying over nothing, really."

Susanne was almost beyond speech by that time. She pointed a finger toward the man as she practically yelled. She stood defiantly with her feet spread and no weakness in her voice. "I have one question for you, Mr. Honest Policeman. How did you know my car was silver? You never asked me to describe it."

"Uh, I must have picked up that piece of the story from my nephew, you know, the store manager."

"Your nephew. This is all becoming very clear to us now. You're both in this together. You have a scam going. I'm going to call the United States Consulate and you'll all be in jail, but you won't be wearing a policía uniform."

"Suit yourselves, señoritas. Either way, you're going to be here for several days. I suggest you go get yourselves a room at the hotel in town and try to relax 'til this all gets worked out. If I can help you anymore, please don't hesitate to come by my office."

"Oh, we'll be in touch. Count on it."

"And señoritas, this is a very small town. I'd be careful about telling people how your car was stolen from you. You never know who might be offended with your unproven allegations. It could cause you further... Let's say, complications. Have a good day."

The greasy looking, grotesquely fat officer smiled broadly as he left the two woman standing beside the road. He made no effort to convince them of his non-involvement.

Susanne and Karen looked at each other incredulously. Susanne couldn't hold it back in any manner. She was hot under the collar and wanted justice, but justice could be very hard to find in an obscure town many hundreds of miles south of the border.

She turned to Karen. "Now what? No car. No bags, which means we have only the clothes on our backs. Thank God we took our purses into the bathroom or they'd have our credit cards and passports as well. We need to get to a phone that isn't under the control of these rats and call somebody to help us."

"I guess we need to head downtown and find that hotel our policía friend was talking about."

The two women started walking down the road. It was even hotter now and it crossed their minds that they would have been a lot better off to have vacationed at home. As they walked down the potholed, two-lane goat path called a highway, they were distracted by a young boy standing outside of a small pueblo type house, just one step off the street. He looked to be around fourteen years old and had on the most worn set of ill-fitting clothes imaginable. He looked like the poster child for third world poverty.

"Did you see that? That boy is waving at us. I'm serious. He wants to speak with us. Think we should walk over there?"

"What's left to steal? If he can speak English, maybe he can tell us where to find another place to stay besides this hotel the cop wants us to stay at. The rooms there are probably on a hidden webcam or something. This whole town gives me the creeps."

Susanne approached the boy. "Yes, what can we do for you?"

"Señoritas, your car was stolen. Am I right?"

"That's correct. How did you know that?"

"I watch them do it. They do this all the time. You need to get out of here as soon as you can. This is not the end of bad things that are going to happen."

"What are you talking about? What else could happen?"

"I'll tell you that but first, come inside. I'm here by myself now and no one will be here 'til tonight. You'll be safe here."

Sensing sincerity from the boy, Susanne and Karen followed him into the very humble dwelling. The house was sparsely furnished with ramshackle pieces that looked as though they had been gathered at the dump. A single light bulb hanging from the ceiling on a cord gave a dim glow throughout the room. In the corner was an antique floor fan, circulating noisily, but at least cooling whomever the breeze hit as it passed by.

"Sit down, señoritas. Can I get you a glass of water?"

"I don't think so, son. Drinking the water down here is not usually a very good thing for Americans to do. Tell us, what do you know about our car? Did you see who took it?"

"I don't have to see it every time. It's always the same people."

"What do they do with them? Do they send them to a chop shop and sell all the parts? Is that what they do?"

"No. They don't even want your car."

"Then why did they steal it?"

"They are going to use it to run drugs across the border. If they get stopped, the driver will just run and all they'll have is your car with the drugs in it. They do it many times a day all along the border. You were just unlucky."

"Do you know where they take them before they use them? Could I get the authorities and go get it back?"

"No, señorita. The authorities are all a part of it. They all make money off the drugs. That's the main way people around here make a living."

"Why are you telling us all this? Aren't you worried they'll punish you?"

"No. I'm not worried. They've already punished me. That's why I'm living here in this dump. My father was a teacher and we lived in another town a long way from here. It happened when I was about eight years old but I still remember. He spoke out against the drug lords during his classes. They came in the middle of the night and killed him. They shot him first and then hung him in the center of town as a warning to everyone else. And my mother, they took her and said she would pay them back working in a brothel for the rest of her life. I never saw her again.

"They sent me here to live with this family that treats me like a slave. I clean their house, milk their cows, mow neighbors' lawns, and give them all the money. Now, they're saying they want to train me to drive cars like yours so they can rent me out to the cartels. I hate them and want out of here. That's why I'm telling you this. I don't have a car. I have no money and don't even know where to go. If you will help me, I will help you. We can save each other.

"These are very bad people and they're not done with you yet. If they were, you'd already be dead and buried in a swamp. I know this for real. They've done it many times already. Life means nothing to El Dorado. He wants only money and power."

"El Dorado? Who's that?"

"He is the owner of the poppy fields. His name means The Golden One. He is one of the richest men in all of Mexico, and the most ruthless. He would just as easily kill you as spit. You don't want to cross him. I would like to kill him for what he did to my family, but now I just want to get away from here and this awful life. Will you help me?"

"I don't know how we can help each other. If what you say is true, then we need to leave as quickly as we can. Our car is gone and we only have a little bit of cash. What do you think we could do if we agreed to help you?"

"I have an uncle who lives on the coast. He is a fisherman and has a boat. I haven't seen him for many years, but he would remember me. If we can get to the coast then he could get us on a boat going to the United States. You are citizens. You could help me get there and stay there. If I can get him to help us, will you take me with you?"

Susanne and Karen stepped aside and discussed his proposition. A decision was quickly reached. "You're on. What's your name?"

"Everyone calls me Triste."

"That means unhappy, doesn't it?"

"That's right. You help me get out of here and you can call me Feliz, because then I'll be happy."

The girls shook hands with Triste to cement their agreement. He had been living this way for over six years. It had been a very degrading and unhappy time for him. He had made his mind up to leave any way he could find, and this was the best chance he'd come across so far. In just moments, he came out of the back room with a very small, beat up gym bag filled with everything he owned. The women introduced themselves to him, and they all left together, walking away from the road that led to the downtown hotel where they were no doubt expected. It was starting to get dark and the women were glad to have Triste along. To have any idea where they were going in the dark would have been impossible without him. Triste led the way.

"There's an old railroad bridge ahead that has a tiny stream running under it. We can hide there until it gets really late and then we'll walk along the stream bank toward the coast. That's where the river goes. Maybe we can catch a bus tomorrow once we're far enough away from here. They won't be looking for me right away because they really don't care about me. You, however, they will be looking for."

"Why would they want us now? They've already got the car."

"You were supposed to go to the hotel. The last couple that lost their car like you went there. Later that evening there was a gas leak in their room and they both died. The town was good enough to bury them in the cemetery. They're still using their social security numbers and credit cards; I guarantee you. No one ever investigates further than what the local police say. It's stupid

to cross El Dorado. He has people everywhere watching out for things. That's why we have to be careful and leave quickly. We can't stop or they'll find us and kill us."

"Lead on Triste. We're trusting you to get us out of here."

"I will. I'm never going back. But one day I will kill El Dorado for what he did to my family. I will never forget. If he dies first, then I'll kill his wife, his kids, his dog. I'll never forget or forgive him. I'm his enemy for life."

Triste had convinced Susanne and Karen that if they were found, their lives would be over. They were tired, hungry, and very scared, but had trusted their future into the hands of a small, fourteen-year-old boy. They found the railroad trestle about 10:00 p.m. and lay down on the hard-rock shoreline of the streambed for about four hours.

5

Triste woke the women at 2:00 a.m. and explained it was time to move. As they started out from under the bridge they heard a car approaching. They hid in the bushes along the shoreline just in time to see an old pickup truck creep slowly down the road alongside the stream. As the vehicle approached the bridge, a handheld spotlight lit up the exact space they had just left moments before. The spot continued to move around the entire area and even passed over the front of the bushes they were currently hiding behind. After a few minutes, the truck moved forward again, all the while shining the light into every conceivable hiding place.

"El Dorado knows you didn't go to the hotel and that you are trying to escape. He will have many men looking for you. We have to be very careful and move as quickly as we can."

"Let's get the hell out of here."

By noon the next day, they had covered about fifteen or twenty miles. Progress was slow as they were constantly trying to stay out of sight of traffic. They saw a small town ahead, and they planned to try to catch a bus to the coast from there. The only problem was that the women would be easily spotted as Americans. They needed to blend in and Triste had an idea.

"I need some cash to buy you both new dresses that look more local. The only place around here that women wear what you have on is television."

The girls searched their pocketbooks thoroughly and came up with a hundred dollars. Triste assured them the dresses would cost no more than ten dollars each. They gave him the money, and he headed into town. When he returned, he had two flower print dresses that looked like they had come out of a scene from a 1940s movie. Karen held one up and remarked with a smile, "I guarantee you that no man will want to catch us wearing these. We're safe now."

Susanne picked up the other one while Triste tried to assure them they were the right choice, "I know they're not pretty, but they only had a couple in the store and the others were worse. You'll look right at home on the bus. If we only had a chicken you could carry no one would ever question you."

Susanne made her opinion very clear regarding the acquisition of livestock. "I'm not holding a live chicken on a bus while I'm dressed like a milk maid and that's final."

As the bus pulled away from the small, dirty stucco building that served as the terminal, Karen and Triste sat like mother and son on one side of the bus, and Susanne sat by herself on the other side, with a vacant seat next to her and the chicken in her lap. As the bus backfired pulling away, the chicken squawked and squirmed as it tried to break Susanne's grip on its legs. Karen looked over at Susanne and smiled. Since they didn't speak Spanish and couldn't give away the fact they were American, a dirty look was all Susanne could give back.

Five and a half hours later, the rusted out, converted school bus arrived at the coastal town of Veracruz. Triste knew his Uncle Eduardo lived in the town and was a fisherman. He had never divulged this during the time he had spent as a virtual slave and hoped that it was still his secret and his alone. The three escapees hurried to the docks. The fishing boats of Veracruz all used the same docks on the south side of the city. There was a protected inlet where they could offload their catch, fuel up, take on provisions, and wait out bad weather. Susanne and Karen remained in their peasant dresses, and Triste bought them each a coffee and pastry that they devoured while sitting on a seawall near the docks. Triste cautiously approached several fishermen and inquired if they knew the whereabouts of his uncle. After several tries, he got an answer, but it was not the one he was hoping for. The girls watched as he walked back toward them, head down, staring at his boots.

"He's dead. The guy I spoke to said he worked for him a couple of years ago and that one morning he didn't show up, and they found him dead in his bed. He had a heart attack or something in his sleep. His old boat is the one with the blue hull over at the end. When he didn't pay the marina bill, they took it for the debt and finally sold it last year. I don't know what to do now."

"Can you find out who bought it? Maybe we could pay him a couple hundred bucks to get us across the Gulf of Mexico. They can't make much fishing. Triste, why don't you go find the guy who owns it now and see if he would like to pick up a few extra bucks hauling passengers?"

"I'll try. I'll check him out first and see what he's like. I can pretend I'm looking for a job, and if he's a good guy, I'll mention I know how he could make some extra money. You stay here, and I'll be back in a little while."

"Here, Triste, before you go, have one of these pastries and a drink."

Triste wolfed down the sugar coated biscuit, drank a soft drink in two long gulps, and took off across the docks. The boat was old but looked well-kept and in order. It had the typical high bow for fishing in big waves and the aft portion had a large, flat deck for a working platform when hauling the nets. There were two young guys mending nets on the stern and an older man sitting in the pilothouse. Triste figured that to be the owner and walked over to the dock beside that portion of the vessel. He called out in Spanish, "Captain, may I come aboard?"

The old man lifted his head up from the chart he was reading and peered over the rail. He saw Triste waving at him from the dock.

"Captain, can I speak with you for just a moment?"

"Sure, kid. Come on up."

Triste climbed the steep steps to the boat's pilothouse and introduced himself to the elderly man.

"What can I do for you?"

"Eduardo was my uncle. He always said I could come work for him when I got old enough, so I came down to see if he would he still take me on. I'm fourteen now and in need of a job. My parents are both dead, and I've got nowhere else to go. Would you need any help? I'm a very hard worker, and I would love to work on a ship like this. My name is Triste."

"I don't know, kid. I've already got two good crew. These boats don't make a lot of money anymore. Between the damn government, taxes, and all the payoffs to bullshit bureaucratic crooks, there ain't much left. How could you help me?"

Just as Triste got ready to finish his sales pitch, they were interrupted by sirens as police cars pulled up nearby. They both looked out the pilothouse window. The police were pulled over right where Triste had left Susanne and Karen.

"Well I'll be damned. Looks like the cops found those two American smugglers they were telling us about yesterday. They were looking all up and down the coast for them. We've got enough drug banditos of our own down here. We sure as hell don't need any illegal aliens coming down here to smuggle drugs back into the States. Glad they got 'em. Now, what were you saying, young man?"

"I will be the best employee you ever had, but I have to run for just a minute. I left my bike by the road over there, and I think I see somebody messing with it. I promise I'll be back."

"Okay, Triste. I'm interested. You come back and we'll see what we can work out."

"Yes, sir."

Triste ran back to the where the police cars where gathered just in time to see the women being loaded into the back of the car. Susanne looked out the window and spotted Triste. She put her finger to her mouth in a signal for him to keep quiet. She was not going to tell the police about him. He was the one person on their side in this Godforsaken country. Triste walked over to one of the remaining policemen and tried to find out where they were taking the women.

"Officer, someone stole my bicycle. It was right here just a short while ago. Did those people you just arrested steal stuff? Maybe they got my bike."

"Sorry, kid. They're drug smugglers. They're big time. Wanted all up and down the coast. Found their car at the border yesterday, loaded with cocaine. They got away there, but we picked them up here. We're not quite as dumb as these Americans like to think we are."

"Where will they take them? Back to the United States?"

"No way. Tonight they'll stay here in the local jail and the police from Mexico City will be here in a special van tomorrow afternoon to pick them up. They said they needed special handling. Didn't look that dangerous. It shows you just can't tell who's a criminal by looking at them. Sorry about the bike, kid."

"No problem. I think I'll go to the police station and file a stolen property report. Where is it?"

"Six blocks down Main Street. Can't miss it. You might not be able to get in there this evening though, what with all the commotion over these drug smugglers."

"Yes, sir. Thanks."

* * *

As the night started to close on Veracruz, a dark hulled sailboat eased into port. *Dark Lady* had completed her crossing of the Gulf of Mexico. With only a compass to steer by, she was quite a bit north of where they had intended to arrive, but that was not a huge problem for anyone on board, as they didn't expect to go to Mexico at all when they had left Florida. They could rest a while, explore the coastal town, and then ease down the coast at their leisure. Bones rounded *Dark Lady* up into the wind so the crew could drop anchor.

"Okay, boys, let her go. This looks like a good spot. I'll back her down on the hook to make sure it's set good. Hawkins, go below and dig the yellow quarantine flag out of the nav station top drawer. We have to let the local thieves know we are here, so they can come aboard and blackmail us to anchor here."

"What are you talking about, Bones?"

"It's the same almost everywhere in the third world. Everybody's poorer than dirt so when they get a government job, such as port authority police, they shake down the visiting boaters for cash. You don't grease their palm a little, you'll definitely have problems getting in or out of the port. They're corrupt, but they do have some power over you, so you have to play their game. They're sort of modern day pirates, if you will. Mexico is a beautiful place and the people are, for the most part, hard-working, kind, and family oriented. The drug business is ruining their heritage and pretty much their entire country. Well, we have to stay onboard 'til we've cleared customs. How about we celebrate with an old Mexican tradition and take a little sip of tequila? I've got a bottle of Mexico's best in my cabin. You boys straighten things up on the topside here, and I'll go fetch the libations."

"Aye, aye, Skipper."

Bones was turning out to be a very able skipper and much smarter than one might guess from their initial conversation. He had a wide breadth of knowledge on a lot of subjects and was interesting to talk to. There was always a feeling in the back of my mind though, that he was holding something back, something that he didn't want to get into with us. I figured he'd open up a little more as we got to know him better.

In short order, we had a nice steel drum tune on the speakers and we were into the devil's brew. In my time, I have found that tequila goes down too easily. So easily, in fact, that one minute, you're sitting around a table talking about politics, science and religion, and thirty minutes later, you're half vegetable and half second grader.

Around eight, we heard an outboard motor approaching us. Shortly thereafter, two uniformed Mexican Port Authority agents stood on the deck wanting to know who the captain of our vessel was. One of them spoke English fairly well, so there was no impediment to understanding what they wanted. We gathered up our passports and handed them to the one who spoke English. He studied each picture and compared it to us individually. He handed them all back to Bones and finally asked the question we were waiting for.

"So, gentlemen. You are here in our country for a good time, am I right? I would like to have a good time, as well. Unfortunately, I have a sick wife and five small children who must eat regularly and visit the doctor. That doesn't leave much dinero for me to have fun with. As embarrassing as it is to me personally, I must depend on the generosity of those who visit my country to subsidize the meager wages the state pays me. Otherwise, my family will starve. I don't suppose you would want to help me and Arturo here who has problems equal to my own?"

Bones reached in his pocket and pulled out a ten-dollar bill. He tried to hand it to the agent who refused to take it. "Señor, do you know of any good doctors who would see a sick bambino for ten dollars? I appreciate your gesture, but to accept it would be to accept an insult. I am, after all, only here to help you and your crew to clear the countless government regulations that could dramatically slow down your movements in our country. Surely, that sort of help is worth more than ten American dollars."

"Well, it might be worth more, but I don't have any more. Maybe my crew here can contribute a little to your health insurance fund. How about it, boys?"

I pulled out my wallet and took out a twenty. David and Tuna did likewise. When Tom started fumbling, trying to reach into his back pocket, it became apparent to us all that he had, perhaps, indulged a little too much in the consumption of the now empty tequila bottle. As he pulled out his wallet, he dropped it onto the deck, and as he picked it up, he made the unfortunate mistake of expressing his feelings. I've heard it said that a drunk man's words are a sober man's thoughts. He definitely said what we were all thinking. "Alright, alright. Give me just a minute here, and I'll get out the blood money to give to this friggin' wetback, two-bit thief. Maybe then, the bastard will leave, and we can go back to our tequila."

"Well, now my friends. I see that we have gone from a pleasant exchange of greetings to a state of disagreement. I'm afraid that I will no longer be able to assist you with the myriad problems that go along with visiting a foreign country. In fact, I'm going to have to take your crewmember here down to our local lockup until he sobers up. You can now do business down at the jail, which I'm sure you'll find is quite a bit more expensive than dealing with me. Arturo, place this gentleman under arrest."

David, Tuna, and I were ready to go to Tom's assistance, throw these bastards into the water and sail back out of the harbor but Bones, in a clear exhibition of understanding the moment, kept us from acting on our thoughts. "Boys, we'll just go down to the jailhouse and pay whatever fine these folks feel like they need and get Tom back. Excuse me, sir, but how long before we can bail out our friend?"

"Captain. There is no guarantee you can bail him out at all tonight. If you think you can be more cooperative with our customs and traditions, you might come by the jail in about an hour or so, and I'll see if some sort of accommodation can be made to release your friend. And Captain, it won't be cheap."

"I understand, completely. By the way, sir..."

"Yes?"

"I'm afraid that our crewman, who obviously likes the bottle a little too much, might come back to the ship and find that I had this very expensive bottle of twelve year old scotch on board. Do you think it would be a good idea if you were to take this for safe keeping?"

"A very good idea, Captain. But you know I might have to pay someone to store it properly since some of the other agents down at the office don't have the integrity that I do and they might be tempted to try some of it themselves. That would be bad. As agents, they could lose their jobs."

"What do you think it might cost to store it?"

"I think something could be arranged for, let's say, one hundred U.S. dollars."

"That sounds reasonable. However, I might have to go get some assistance to raise that amount of money. Tell you what, I'll give you half now and half when we come down to pick up our crewman. How much money do you think his bail will be?"

"I think, my friend, you show up at the station with fifty more dollars for liquor storage and another hundred for bail and your friend will be quickly on his way back to your ship."

"Thank you, sir, for your understanding in this matter."

"Captain, understanding all the ramifications of these matters is my job. I'll see you shortly at the station."

"Yes, sir."

If it weren't such a serious matter, it would have been almost comical to watch all six feet six of Tom being escorted to their car in handcuffs by these two short, fat corrupt jerks.

Normally a very polished professional, Tom was too inebriated to deal with them tonight. They were lucky that he wasn't sober or taking him away could have been extremely difficult. I, for one, would never want to upset him.

When they left, Bones laid out his plan. "All right, boys. We've gotten into somewhat of a sticky wicket here. They're holding all the aces right now, so we're going to have to do what they say or it will only get worse. I've heard plenty of stories of folks being held for ransom by the authorities down here. Money is the only law in Mexico. We need to come up with another hundred fifty bucks pronto. How are you fellas fixed for cash?"

We all dug deep into our wallets, even the parts behind the hidden leather flap. We had enough between us and a few bucks to spare. Bones continued, "Here's what we need to do. I've dealt with a lot of these types before. It's not complicated, but you have to take precautions. Me and Hawkins here will go to the jail to get our man. Salmon can stay behind and watch out for *Dark Lady*."

"That's Tuna, not Salmon."

"Okay, whatever. You know who you are. One thing they like to do is get you off your boat and then steal everything from it that's not nailed down. So, Squid, you stay up on deck where they can see you and more than likely they won't even try to come aboard."

"What happens if they do?"

"If they ain't armed, cuss at 'em and raise a loud ruckus. If they are carrying heat, jump off the other side of the boat and swim to shore. That's about the best advice I can give you. That's what I'd do."

"That doesn't sound like much fun. What the heck? You guys go get Tom and then let's get the hell out of here."

Bones turned toward me and half smiled as he handed out instructions on how to accomplish the mission. In truth, he didn't appear to be at all frightened of the prospect that things might not go as planned. I assumed his time in Vietnam must have steeled him to this sort of endeavor. His sense of calm was impressive.

"Now Hawkins, you and David take off your watches and jewelry and leave anything on the boat that's valuable. They see you wearing a nice watch and suddenly they'll need one to tell what time to let your man go. You get my drift?"

"We do."

"Okay, then. Let's head on over to the jail. By the time we row to shore and walk that far, the hour will be up, and I don't want to give them any more time to try to figure some more ways to screw us. Let's go."

We scurried down the rope ladder to the dinghy and left a nervous Tuna behind. We tied up behind a very downtrodden seafood warehouse on the waterfront and started walking toward the center of town. It was not an unpleasant looking place, though it didn't offer much in the way of cleanliness. The storefronts were stucco and painted in Caribbean pastels. A number of people were sitting in chairs on the sidewalks and Latin rhythms were blaring out of more than one bar. Prior to this evenng's events, I would have liked to stop in a few of these places.

The jail was not hard to find. Out in front were a number of policía and several beat up squad cars. We checked the time on the wall clock as we walked in and we were exactly one hour as requested. The agent who blackmailed us saw us as we entered and walked over to Bones as if he was greeting an old friend he hadn't seen in months.

"Ah, Captain. Good to see you. I see you've come for your man. He's in good shape, though he's sleeping quite soundly in the cell. You have his bond as we asked?"

"Right here." Bones showed the officer the cash.

"Very good. I'll take that, you sign his release document, and you are free to take him. But I caution you, don't let him get in trouble again while you are here or he will have to face the judge next time, who's not nearly so easily negotiated with as I was. Now, you can go get him up."

He called to a guy in the back who must have been the jailer and told him to unlock Tom's cell. I went in and found him as the policeman said I would, dead to the world on a bunk. "Tom, come on buddy. You've got to get up now. Time to go home." I shook his shoulders and forced him to sit up in the bunk. He was going to have one hell of a hangover.

"Where am I? Geez, this looks like a jail cell."

"It is. You got into a little argument with the port agent and they brought you here. It's all right now. We paid a fine and you're free to leave."

"Man, I'm sorry. That tequila just laid me out. I'll never touch that stuff again. I must be allergic to it. Oh crap, I feel like I need to throw up. I need a pail or something."

I motioned for the jailer. He spoke no English, so I pointed at Tom, who was gagging. The jailer pointed down the hall to the next room. He made a gesture with his hand like he was flushing a toilet. I helped Tom up and we started back there. I noticed as we entered the next room that there were more cells and one of them had two young women in it. Tom went into the toilet and I shut the door behind him. I stood in the hall between two cells. One of the women motioned quietly to me. "We're Americans. Are you American?"

"Yes. Are you okay?"

"No. They are framing us, and tomorrow a drug guy is going to send people to pick us up, and then they're going to kill us. Please, for God's sake, help us get out of here. You are our only hope. These people are all crooks. They're all in the drug business. They told us we'll be dead tomorrow. They're not joking. You've got to help us."

"What can I do?"

"I don't know. I've never been in jail before. But we don't want to die. You've got to help us."

"I need a little time to come up with something. I'll be back. We won't let them do anything to you."

"Thank you. Thank you."

I could hear Tom throwing up just inside the door. I looked around the room and tried to come up with some plan to help these girls. I didn't doubt for a minute what these police officers were capable of. We'd seen it first-hand. This was not the sort of adventure I had been looking for and by this time, my pulse had to be hitting overdrive. I tried to mimic Bones' calm demeanor and forget the immediate danger. The jailer's desk was just inside a small cubicle-sized office at the end of the hall, right beside the bathroom Tom was occupying. I could see the jailer reading the paper and there was a set of keys hanging on a hook right above the desk. I told Bones what I was thinking about trying to do.

"We've got to help those ladies or they're going to kill them. There's a set of keys just over the desk in the jailer's office. If you can get Tom to act really sick and maybe clog up the toilet so that it starts to overflow, I'll get the guy to go in there to help. Then I'll borrow his keys just long enough to unlock the girl's cell door."

"Then what?"

"I'm thinking about the next step, but we've got to get the door unlocked before anything else can be done. Get Tom to start puking."

Bones joined Tom in the bathroom and in just a few minutes, the most disgusting sounds emanated from that room. I heard the toilet flush four times and then saw the water seeping out from under the door. The door opened and Bones and Tom stepped out. Bones called for the jailer and showed him what was happening. He cursed a number of times, opened a broom closet beside the toilet, and retrieved a mop. Tom, David, and Bones stood between him and me, apologizing all the while. As the jailer continued his cussing, I took the opportunity to grab the keys and, after two incorrect tries, found the right match. I whispered to the girls.

"Don't leave yet. I'm putting the keys back up. They won't know anything. You'll know when to leave. We'll give you a signal. It won't be too long. Just stay tuned."

"What's the signal?"

"I don't know yet. Maybe I'll just whistle real loud. Yes, that's what I'll do. You run out as quickly as you can and we'll be waiting for you. Don't hesitate at all. Got it?"

"We do. And mister, what's your name?"

"Jim."

"Thank you, Jim. We'll never forget this."

"Neither will I."

Triste was waiting and watching just outside the jail. He was trying to find a way to get Susanne and Karen out before El Dorado's men came for them. He wanted to create a distraction that would empty the entire jail, but was finding it difficult to formulate a plan. He saw the two squad cars sitting right in front of the jail and noticed that one had the windows open. If he could create a very loud problem with that car, they would certainly come outside to see what was happening.

At the same time, Bones, Tom, David, and I were walking out together. I looked both ways down the quiet street and saw only a city bucket truck with the arm extended and a worker making adjustments to an antique streetlight. Obviously, I had never planned a jailbreak before, so I was in new territory. I turned to the guys.

"Tom, are you recovered enough to stick with us if we start to run down the street?"

"Yeah, I'm feeling a lot better since I got that crap out of my stomach. I'll be all right. Just tell us what you have in mind."

"I don't know how all this is going to play out, but we've got to try. David, I'm going to go stand near the door to the jail. When I give you a signal, you hit the siren in that squad car and hold it 'til you see the ladies run out of the door. Bones, you and Tom steer the ladies down the street to the boat as fast as you can go. We'll catch up to you. Here goes nothing."

As nonchalantly as I could, I walked up to the door. Inside the front office were our favorite customs agent and one other policeman. The jailer was in the back. I looked over toward David and gave him a wave. He fumbled around for over a minute 'til he found the right switch. Finally, the siren started wailing. I looked inside and saw the two men in the front office start toward the door, and the jailer stuck his head out the door of his cubicle. They were cussing and no doubt thinking that some kids were playing with their equipment. Just as they exited the door and looked over to where David was sitting in the squad car, there was a huge explosion. I looked toward the explosion and saw their other squad car burst into a ball of fire like a bomb went off inside it. The policemen immediately changed directions and ran toward the burning car. Two seconds later, the jailer came out of the front door to see what all the commotion was about. I slipped inside as he passed by and gave a low whistle. I watched, but they didn't come out. I whistled again to no avail and finally I had to go deeper inside the building. I went to their cell, and there they stood.

"Didn't you hear me? I've been whistling my butt off."

"I'm sorry, we couldn't be sure it was whistling with all the screaming, the sirens, and explosions."

"Well, come on. Quick! Follow me."

We ran out of the front door of the jail and saw the two officers and the jailer trying to put out the fire. With the wind blowing sparks everywhere, there was a real danger that it might set the entire jailhouse on fire. The jailer wrapped a coat around his arm and in a brave gesture, reached through the window and shifted the old car into neutral. All three officers then put a foot on the back bumper of the car and pushed it away from the curb. Things didn't go quite like they had expected. The burning car picked up speed as it moved down a slight hill and slammed into the back of the bucket truck, which then proceeded to fall over and drop the bucket arm onto the wires and cables holding the streetlight in place. The workman scrambled down the mechanical arm as it was falling and then the light, with its cable broken on one side of the street, swung over to the other side and proceeded to go through the front window of a small bar. Immediately, the bar patrons emptied out into the street. Thinking World War III had broken out; they began screaming and going berserk. It looked like a scene from a *Keystone Kops* movie. As we watched, the women saw one of the police grab Triste and smell his shirt. Even in Spanish it was easy to understand that he said *gasoline*. They had discovered who started the inferno. Frantically, Susanne grabbed my arm as I started toward freedom, "We've got to help him! The boy did this to free us, and we can't just let them have him. If they'll kill women, I don't doubt they'll do the same to a kid."

The entire scene was surreal. I couldn't believe I was an integral part to all of this chaos. With no other choices presenting themselves at that moment, I walked over to the cops and said, "He's with us. I'll take him home and punish him severely."

"You again? You are absolutely crazy. You and your crew are all going back to jail and this young punk with you. The jailer pulled his gun from its holster and pointed it at my chest. He never saw it coming when Susanne cracked him over the head with a fire extinguisher. David, having hot-wired the other squad car, backed it up, and the women, Triste, two officers and I all piled in. I held the gun on them in the back seat while David, the girls and Triste sat on each other's laps in the front. The one officer who spoke English started rattling on about how much trouble we were in and how we'd never get away with this. I felt a little like Dirty Harry by that time. My inner machismo was showing for perhaps the first time in my entire life. It felt good to make a stand against evil.

"You need to understand who's holding the *pistoli* and shut the hell up! I'm already pretty upset, and this gun could go off real easily."

"No, señor. Be very careful. Please, señor."

"Then sit still and keep your mouths shut. Where's Bones and Tom?"

David knew their plan. "They've gone to the boat. Bones said to meet them at the pier. They're going to weigh anchor and meet us at the dock. We won't have to make trips back and forth with the dinghy."

The cop who couldn't keep his mouth shut volunteered again, "You expect to get away in a boat? A sailboat? You people are insane."

"What part of shut-up do you have trouble understanding?"

In only a minute, we were at the dock, and just as Bones said would happen, *Dark Lady* pulled alongside the pier. We parked the squad car in an alley, so it wouldn't be found instantly, and we all boarded the boat with the two policemen in our custody. They were shaking their heads in disbelief.

"You people are loco. You are now kidnapping a federal officer of the country of Mexico. This could cause a war between the United States and Mexico."

"That would be fun. Half our soldiers are your countrymen trying to get citizenship."

"Where are you taking us? Are you going back to Florida? I'd be okay with Florida. So would my friend here. I'd like Tampa. Can you drop me off in Tampa?"

"Shut the hell up. You're making my trigger finger itch again."

With no running lights and the motor at just above idle speed, Bones steered *Dark Lady* toward the entrance of the channel to make our escape. He turned the wheel over to David and came to where I was holding the police officers. He didn't seem to have any concern whatsoever with who and what they were.

"As much as we'd like to take you with us and as much as I'm sure you'd like to go, we can't take you to Florida."

"Where will you let us off?"

"We're almost there."

"Where?"

"Buoy number three. Right at the entrance to the harbor. The tide is coming in, so you'll drift right to shore in a couple hours or so."

"A couple of hours. Señor, I can't swim. I'll drown."

"No you won't. We'll do you better than you would have done us. We'll put a life jacket on each of you, and you can dog paddle back to shore. Drowning won't be an issue. Now sharks, that's another thing altogether. I don't know how bad they are around here. Do you?"

"No, señor, no. Please, I'm afraid of the water and sharks. There could even be crocodiles. Please don't do this."

Bones wasn't smiling anymore. "You're going to have a lot more than sharks and crocs to worry about tomorrow when your drug gang buddies show up to retrieve the two innocent women you were willing to see killed. I don't think they're going to be very pleased when they hear you let them escape. Now, stick out your arms or you won't have a life jacket. You don't want to try and make shore without one, I'm certain."

The two officers extended their arms and Bones put a life vest on each of them. He then walked them over to the rail and pushed each of them overboard. His actions were remarkably nonchalant. Bones definitely had a very hard side to him. I now knew he was not a man to cross.

"I figure they'll be ashore in a couple of hours, so we need to make tracks. We'll motor sail to make as much time as we can. The U.S. Coast Guard patrols most of the Gulf, so they won't follow us but so far. It'll be dark for another eight hours. We can be a long way offshore by then. We'll be all right. Okay, boys, sail ho!"

Relief was plastered all over Susanne's and Karen's faces. They gathered around their young hero Triste and got his version of the escape. He said he had surveyed the jail and realized there was no way possible for him to get inside to free them. He figured that if a car just outside the building were to catch fire putting the building at risk, they'd have to come outside, and perhaps then he could help the girls make a break for it. He had no idea how successful his plan would become. He had caused more problems in thirty seconds than he had ever imagined.

Bones steered *Dark Lady* toward the open waters of the Gulf of Mexico and we sailed without lights throughout the night to make our position less obvious, in case anyone was trying to locate us. David kept watch to our stern looking for vessels that might be approaching; if other ships couldn't see us, we certainly needed to see them in order to avoid a collision.

6

As things calmed down onboard, we gathered around the two women and their young friend to find out a little about the people we had just helped escape from what would have been a certain death.

"I'm Jim Hardison, this is Tom Joseph and Jim Fortuna. Bones is the guy on the wheel, and David Pfefferkorn is keeping watch on the stern. We're from North Carolina and went to Florida to charter a boat to the Bahamas for a sailing vacation. Through a pretty wild set of circumstances, we wound up as Bones' crew for a couple of weeks. We never intended to wind up in Mexico, but the weather sort of brought us in this direction. What's your story?"

"I'm Susanne and this is my best friend Karen. We were heading to Cozumel for a vacation and got our car stolen by some gang members wanting to use it to run drugs across the border. Of course, if they got busted, it was my car and they would love nothing more than to frame two women from the States. That would be us. Triste has been our savior for the past couple of days. He was orphaned by the same bunch of thugs and their boss, the great and mighty El Dorado. They are the worst people on the planet. If it weren't for Triste, we'd already be dead. We're going to do what we can to help him. Where are you guys headed?"

"Well, that's kinda up in the air right now. We wanted to head east to the Bahamas, but the wind didn't cooperate with us. We went to the Dry Tortugas and snorkeled but when we tried to leave, the only direction that was good sailing brought us here."

"Thank God for a foul wind. If you guys hadn't shown up, Karen and I might not be breathing right now. Do you think we're safe out here?"

"I hope so. I've never been around anyone like this drug gang, but I've certainly heard about some of their atrocities on the news. I wouldn't put anything past them and I'm sure the last thing they want is for their intended victims to get away and talk to the authorities about what happened. Not good publicity for the Mexican government's image either, not that it's very good now. So to answer your question, I think we need to be very careful where we go and what we do for a while. We don't want to cross paths with any of them again."

Susanne and Karen went below to take a well-deserved shower and get some rest. Triste was too excited to go to bed and asked if he could walk around the deck of *Dark Lady*. I explained to him the need to walk carefully and showed him where the life vests were stored for quick retrieval if it got rough. It was fairly calm right then, so I felt it was reasonably safe for him to walk about.

David, Tom, Tuna, and I sat together near the stern rail and breathed a collective sigh of relief that our adventure in Veracruz had come to an end. Tom looked over at me. "Dang, Jim. You really showed your colors back there. I didn't think you had that in you."

"You're not the only one. I guess if I'd taken time to think about what I was doing, I'd probably have messed my pants. I know one thing for sure. I don't want to do anything like that again. I'm not cut out to pretend I'm in an episode of 'Cops.'"

"Just the same, you guys all saved my butt."

Tom raised his beer-filled fist. "To great friends and sailors. I'm mighty proud to be sailing with ye!"

We all raised our beers in response. "Cheers."

It was a beautiful moonlit evening. The wind had moved around to the southeast, just enough to let us clear the Yucatan peninsula, south of us. We were on a tight reach, sailing into the wind. *Dark Lady* would make slow progress. Vessels like her were never known for their ability to sail in the direction the wind was coming from. A tight reach was not their best point of sail. We hoped by sunrise we would be well out to sea and a long way from Veracruz. As we talked, I watched Triste wander curiously around the deck. I could only imagine how hard living had been for someone so young who had endured so much in his short life. In spite of everything, he still seemed to have that thirst for life and learning that most young people share. Within an hour, he had eased up beside Bones to watch him steer *Dark Lady*. Both had found something they needed. Triste had someone to learn from and Bones had someone to tell his tales to. They were the perfect audience for each other. We stayed up very late enjoying the spectacle that we were an integral part of. Here we were on a beautiful night, sitting outside on the deck of a turn-of-the-century sailing ship, silently slipping along the Gulf of Mexico just as other sailing vessels had done for hundreds of years. It was special for all of us. As we stared out on the starlit seas, I kept glancing at Bones, who was delicately manipulating the varnished wooden wheel, his hands caressing the glossy curve of its spine, his ever-present pipe, its bowl glowing, and the occasional bit of wisdom he willingly offered up to his young attendant. If our voyage had ended the next morning, it might have been a perfect sail. None of us could see beyond the bow wave *Dark Lady* was pushing up as we made a straight course away from the coast of Mexico. The resort areas of Cancun and Cozumel are on the Yucatan peninsula and stick out into the Gulf of Mexico. To clear them, we had to beat into the wind as tightly as we could. It would be a horse race. We didn't want to get within sight of land under any circumstances.

Dawn found us about eighty miles to sea. The seas were starting to kick up a little bit, but the wind was strong and we were making good time. Unfortunately, the ladies were not sailors and the movement of the boat had taken its toll on them. Susanne was starting to get used to the motion, but we were afraid that Karen was heading for a bout of seasickness. I'd been there before and felt bad for her. I brought her some ginger cookies from the galley, as they seem to have a calming effect on the stomach. She appreciated the gesture, but was having trouble holding them down.

"Hopefully, we'll be out of the chop in a few more hours. Why don't you just lie down on the deck? The temperature is nice today and it's never good to be below when you're having this sort of problem. The horizon remains horizontal and helps you get your bearings. Below, everything is in motion and it makes it difficult to recover. Try to sleep it off."

"I'm trying, but I feel awful."

"I know. It's bad, but you will get over it."

Susanne walked over and asked Karen if she could do anything for her, but it seemed that this was a battle she would have to fight all by herself. This was the first time since we met the two ladies I got to take a closer look at Susanne. I wasn't just a sailor; I was also a man and I had to admit that she had the sort of looks I was attracted to. She was dark haired with olive skin, had a great smile and, even without makeup, she was very striking. Ever since my divorce, my love life had consisted of looking at beautiful boats and imagining how it would be to sleep in one. The divorce had been so brutal that whenever anyone asked me if I was seeing another woman, I gave them the same answer. Once you've been bitten by a cobra, you lose the urge to play with snakes. I knew it was a callous answer, but the fact was I was very bitter. I hadn't done anything wrong in my first marriage other than marry the one person on the planet who couldn't stand me. How had that happened? I really don't know. I had broken up with my first great love in college and was on the rebound. A cute, shy, sweet woman showed me a little attention and I jumped. Unfortunately, she was cute and shy but the sweet washed out pretty fast after we married. Then I discovered that she had a mean streak that would scare a crocodile. I was literally afraid to come home from work the last two years we were together for fear of the tongue-lashing I knew she would be dishing out the minute I arrived. She was the master craftsman of unhappiness, and I was her workbench.

That was all behind me now, along with everything I'd accumulated during our twenty-eight years together. I had three grown kids and a couple of grandkids that I loved dearly. They now had lives of their own, and I had to rebuild mine. That's what got me to the deck of *Dark Lady*, staring at this lovely creature. I had to qualify her regarding boats immediately. I would never consider having anything to do with a woman who didn't love boats and the sea.

"Have you ever been on a sailboat before?"

"My brother had a Hobie Cat when we were young, and I went out with him a couple of times. I remember it was fast and wet. We were kids. It was a lot of fun, but nothing like this. This boat is huge. Is it yours?"

"No. I couldn't begin to afford something like this. It belongs to

Bones over there on the wheel. It's like a part of him. He used to work for the guy that owned it who eventually willed it to him. It's been his home for decades. We just signed on as crew 'cause it's too big for him to sail without help, and we just wanted to go sailing. You know? Have some fun, sun, and adventure. So far, we're having a little too much of the last part of the wish list. I'm for laying back, listening to some soft Caribbean tunes and drinking a few beers. What do you and Karen want us to do for you? I'm sure you don't want us to let you off in Mexico."

"I'm for heading back to Florida with you guys, if Bones will let us tag along. We're from Texas, but if we can get back to the States, we can sure as hell make it home. We don't know anything about sailing this boat, but we can help with the cooking while we learn. What do you say?"

"I'm fine with it. Of course, it's Bones' boat, so we'll need to run it past him. Why don't we do that right now?"

"Lead on."

We joined Bones and Triste at the wheel. Steering a boat the size of *Dark Lady* was work requiring concentration and a feel for the movement of the boat on the water. Nonetheless, Bones never seemed to tire of it.

"Bones, the ladies have a proposition they want to make you. I'll let Susanne speak for the both of them since Karen is having a bout of *mal de mer*."

I enjoyed watching Susanne make her proposal. She had an absolutely lovely smile, and she knew it. With her eyes sparkling and enthusiasm all over her face, she played old Bones like a Stradivarius.

"Mr. Bones."

"Just Bones is fine, darlin.'"

"Bones, it is. Now Bones, Karen and I obviously don't want to be dropped off anywhere near Mexico. I never want to go there again and neither does Karen. Since you and your crew are going home
to Florida, we'd love to become part of your operation. We'd be glad to cook and help you keep your yacht nice. We don't know much about boats, but we're quick learners and we aren't afraid of much. We would definitely not be a burden in any way." Then with a huge smile, she poured it on really thick, "Besides, a big, strong captain such as you needs to have something a little more feminine to look at than these burly old crew members you have now."

Susanne and Karen

"She's good, Hawkins. Real good. And she's got a good point there about needing some help in the galley. You fellas ain't much down there. My appetite goes through the roof when I'm at sea. As a matter of fact, I'm getting a little hungry right now. So, Missy, I'm not opposed to your offer, but what say we do a little test right now of your prowess in the galley? Show us what you can do."

"You won't be disappointed, Bones. Cooking is one of my many passions."

As she said the word passions, I could have sworn she looked my way and gave me a little smile. I wasn't sure there was anything to it other than her enlisting a little more support for her proposal, but I enjoyed the thought just the same. It had been a very long time since any woman had looked my way while using the word passion. It was thought provoking and I sure was thinking.

Susanne went below and I walked back over to Bones and Triste. As I approached, I was very surprised to hear Bones conversing with Triste in perfect Spanish. It was apparent that there were many things about Bones that none of us knew. Even though he conversed easily and often with everyone, he knew how to keep the things he wanted to remain private, private. It made me wonder how much private stuff there was. He was a man of mystery.

By then, we had cleared the point of the Yucatan peninsula and were heading south. If we kept heading in this direction, we would soon be past the west coast of Cuba. With our recent adventure in Veracruz, there was no way we would risk visiting Cancun or Cozumel. Also, time was a factor for most of us, as we had jobs waiting back home, and at some point very soon, we needed to think about turning in a direction that would get us headed back home. I, for one, needed to get home in another week and we were a long way from Florida at the moment.

"Bones, what's the plan now? You realize that we all need to get back home in a week, don't you?"

"Well, Hawkins. I wasn't exactly sure what all of your schedules were, but I think I heard something about two weeks early on. Of course, old Mother Nature ain't been working with us too good up 'til this point. Can't get this old girl to point much higher than what we're doing right now. She's giving us all she's got."

"Then what are you thinking? If we just keep heading south, we'll wind up in South America. If we don't get home on time, we'll all be in trouble at work."

"Work. Never cared too much for punching a clock or having some clown looking over my shoulder all day to see was he getting his ration of blood out of me. You might want to think about living a little like I do. I don't ask nobody when I can come and go. It ain't natural. Might as well work on an old plantation and have an overseer. And when you pass on, don't have to worry about going to heaven, 'cause you sold your soul early on. You need to think about that Hawkins."

Tom, David, and Tuna were now all on deck and they had some questions of their own that were very similar to mine. Tom and David confirmed their schedule was the same as mine. Tuna, on the other hand, was head of research at his firm and had the ability to set his own schedule. He could stretch out his vacation a few days without setting off any fireworks. However, he did have some questions he felt were pertinent to our situation.

"Captain Bones. I've been looking over our electronics that the lightning strike took out. I think I can jury rig a couple of them and perhaps get them going again, maybe not. Time will tell. What I really don't understand is how the devil you know where we are? The GPS is out; you haven't taken a reading with a sextant and you seem to just use the old binnacle compass and your dead reckoning. I don't see how you can know within a hundred miles where we are. How do you keep us from running aground or hitting a reef? I'm at a loss for how you do that. We appear to be just constantly heading south and with the speed the boat is running, we are a very long way from home. I'm fine with that for the time being, but just where is it that you're taking us?"

"Jupiter my friend."

"We're headed to Jupiter. The only Jupiter I know of is Jupiter Inlet in Florida. What Jupiter are you talking about?"

"I'm talking about that one, right up there." Bones pointed a finger skyward.

"If you can pick out Jupiter, the brightest star in the southern sky, then you can head south. This ain't rocket science, Tuna. Sailors have been steering by the stars for thousands of years. You don't think Columbus had a GPS, do you? Folks are too dependent on that modern fan-dangled stuff. You get a lightning strike like we did and guess what? You won't know where the Hell you are. No, sir. The stars have been in the sky for millions of years and I reckon I can count on them remaining where they are, at least 'til I'm done with 'em. Now, what else you fellas needing to know?"

I spoke up. "Bones, I guess what we all want to know is what you are thinking. I know the time doesn't matter to you, but we're all on a schedule of sorts. We're a little flexible, but I don't see how we can keep sailing away from Florida much longer."

"Boys, there's airports in Belize if you need to rush home."

"Belize! You're sailing to Belize? Why are we heading that far south? What's in Belize?"

The conversation that took place next stays in my mind as clear as any picture I've ever seen. We were all looking at Bones and the cobalt blue seas off to our starboard. It was a beautiful place to be. The wind was strong and steady. Bones looked down at his young companion, Triste.

"Okay, son, think you can hold us on course? This here's your chance to steer the *Dark Lady*. See how the rising sun is almost even with the right side of the boat?"

"Yes, sir."

"You keep it right there and that's the course we need to be on. I'll let you know if it changes."

"Alright, Captain Bones. You can count on me."

"That was never in doubt, son. You will be fine crew. Now, boys, let's go over to the stern rail and have a little conversation. I've been wanting to talk with you all for a couple of days about this, and I guess there's no better time than now."

"Talk about what? What is it?"

Bones reached in his pants pocket and pulled out a small pouch of tobacco he kept on the ready for his pipe. He poured a bit into the pipe's bowl and tamped it down ever so gently with his index finger. As if time meant nothing to any of us, he slowly relit his pipe, took two or three long draws from it, and then leaned casually against the stern rail as he spoke.

"Well, boys, you've been a good crew. We've had a few really nice days, especially there in the Tortugas. Been wanting to get back there for years. Mexico, well, it's still Mexico, beautiful and completely corrupt. Been that way for as long as I can remember. I still love it but it's a dangerous place. We could have had some fun there if it hadn't been for our little run-in with the policía. 'Course, if that hadn't happened, we wouldn't have picked up our new crewmembers and I'm really looking forward to some home-cooked meals. Haven't had fried chicken since I can't remember. Love it. Anyway, where was I? Oh yeah. You want to know where the *Dark Lady* is pointed. Good question. I can answer it with one word. One very exciting word and, my friends, that word is 'treasure.'"

How did I know that was what he was going to say? "Geez, we've wound up on the *Hispaniola.* Please tell us you're joking, Bones."

"I can't, boys. I'm as serious as a waterspout. Not too far from where we are right now there is more gold, silver and jewels of every sort than you can possibly dream of."

"Let me finish that for you, Bones. You won a map in a poker game from a guy with an eye patch and a peg leg, no offense on the leg part."

"You can say what you will, boys, but it's all for real. No one could have dreamed up what I'm about to tell you. You know who Mel Fisher was, don't you?"

"Yeah. He owns the pirate museum in Key West, right?"

"It's not a pirate museum; it's a treasure museum. He discovered the wrecks of the Spanish Armada, a treasure fleet headed back to Spain after looting Mayan temples in Mexico. They got caught by a hurricane in the Florida Straits and all of their ships were lost. Mel found the wreck of seven of them including the *Atocha*. He recovered over a billion dollars of treasure."

"Okay, that's Mel Fisher. How does that affect Bones and company?"

"It's funny how you tried to make fun of me about winning the map in a poker game."

"Because you did?"

"Not me, but Nathan Hibbs was in a session one night with several members of Mel's crew. One of the crew said he had a map and used it as collateral. Nathan won it. The hand wasn't but five hundred dollars strong. Nathan always said he thought it was real, but didn't want to make a big deal out of it 'cause he was good buddies with Mel. He always told me he had the map, but never showed it to me. About six years ago, I was replacing some old paneling behind the liquor cabinet in the master stateroom, you know, my quarters on *Dark Lady,* when I pulled it off the wall to set it down, this old map fell out. I knew right off what it was. I'm telling you, it's real and it shows plain as the nose on my face where the rest of the fleet is. Mel knew. He was going there after he finished salvaging the *Atocha*. He never lived to see the plan through. You know, even with that much treasure, he had money problems. Mel was not the best businessman, but he was a genius at salvaging. There's even stories out there that he sold more than a hundred percent of the shares of the company trying to get funding to keep the operation going. Nonetheless, I've got the only copy of the map, and I want to go after the gold. I'm not a greedy man. I just want to live out my remaining days in comfort, maybe travel a little on a plane, not on an old boat that I have to find help to even use. I'd also like to get me a little house in Marathon, right on the Gulf where I can look out over the water when I get too old to take my own boat out. With the gold that's to be found on this map, I could do that times a thousand and all you boys could quit work the next day after we go get it. You interested?"

"You know this all sounds pretty wild, Bones."

"I know it does. Too wild for me to have made up, don't you agree?"

"I don't doubt you're being truthful with us, but just because you have a map you believe in, doesn't mean the map is really legitimate. And even if it is, by your own words, Mel Fisher took many years to salvage the gold off the *Atocha*."

"That's what so great about this map, boys. This treasure ain't on the bottom of the Gulf of Mexico. The story goes that three of the boats that were never found survived, at least initially. Two of them lost their rigs so they took what they could from each of them and jury-rigged the one that was in the best shape. It was named *Pequeña Princesa*. That means little princess in Spanish. They loaded all the treasure on her and went the way the wind blew them, just like we did a few days ago. Only, the wind blew them a lot more to the south than it did us. Have you ever heard of the Turneffe Islands?"

"No. Where are they located?"

"Just off the coast of Belize. It's not in the Gulf of Mexico, my friend. It's in the Caribbean Sea. The islands off the coast of Belize are the most beautiful tropical islands in the world. Whenever you see a picture of a small island with pristine white sand beaches, crystalline blue waters and tall, perfect palms, it's more than likely off Belize. I'm telling you, even if there weren't no gold there, it's worth the trip.

"Anyway, the *Princesa* limped down to an island there that's called Ambergris Caye. She was taking on water badly by the time they got there. Remember, back then, there was nothing on these islands 'cept iguanas and a few primitive Indian tribes. They were afraid the ship would sink, so they offloaded the gold and started to make her seaworthy for the trip back to the mainland. There's no water to drink on most of these islands, and they was running out of food. They got to arguing about who was going to sail the boat to Belize, and who would stay with the gold. Sides got chosen pretty quickly and several fights broke out. Before it was over, almost all of them were dead or badly wounded leaving barely enough of them to even sail the *Princesa* to the mainland. They left two men with the gold 'cause they wanted to make sure no one else found it, not even the Indians. There wasn't any way for them to leave the island, so they felt confident they would watch over the gold and be there when they got back. They found a really good spot to store the treasure. Without my map, you would never locate it – completely impossible. Anyway, they would sail to Belize, repair the *Princesa*, get some supplies and come back for the two men and the treasure. On the way back they got hit with another bad storm and the *Princesa* started to break up. Four of the men made it to a longboat and began to row for all they were worth. Nine days later, one man was found clinging to the overturned longboat about four miles from the coast of Belize. He was delirious and hallucinating, raving madly about gold and emeralds and all the dead sailors he watched go to a watery grave. They took him to a local mission where they nursed him 'til he died. No one ever went back for the two men on the island, so they were toast as well."

"What about the map? Where did that come from?"

"The last sailor, Pierre Salvos, lived at a mission for about a year before he finally gave up the ghost. Just before he died, he gave a nun his one possession: an old handheld compass that he had used to head west to the coast of Belize. It was about the size of a train conductor's pocket watch. The nun thought it was very special since it had been given to her, and it was all the old sailor had owned in the entire world when he died. She kept it for almost sixty years, and when she died, she left it to the mission.

"Some years later, the mission was run by a priest that had a problem with the bottle. The mission fell into disrepair and they finally gave him the boot. He wound up in Texas looking for the next bottle. He swapped the compass, which he had taken when he left, for a bottle of whiskey.

"Later, Mel bought the compass from the great, great grandson of the barkeep. He could spot an old ship's compass in his sleep. He didn't buy it thinking there was a map in it, but when he tried to correct the compass reading to true north, he took it apart. Mel was a lot more than a treasure hunter. He was a true marine archeologist. Anything old that came from a boat was a treasure to him and he wanted it. When he took apart that old compass, that's when he found the map. A few minutes studying it and he understood exactly what he had. The map disappeared with the firing of the worthless crewman who liked to play poker.

"That's the entire history of how Nathan Hibbs came to own the map. I've checked out the story every way I could. Spoke with the curator in Mel's museum, talked with his crewmembers over a whiskey bottle, and listened to every piece of gossip about him. I'm totally convinced it's real.

"The island it's on is small and sparsely inhabited to this day. You fellas help me get it, and I'll be happy with thirty percent. You all can split up the rest however you want. We'll all be filthy rich. Are you with me?"

"You're asking quite a lot to go out on such a limb. We've all heard the stories about treasure maps and lost pirates' gold since we were kids. It's always been part of a Disney movie, so you can understand our hesitation. I think I'd want to see the map and judge for myself if it's real. How about you guys? Tom? David? Tuna?"

Tom spoke up. "If we all think it's real, I'm open to going along at least a while, 'til we come to some sort of group decision on whether we're on a wild goose chase or not. What about you? David? Tuna?"

David said he'd go along with the group at least for a few more days. Tuna was the most reluctant. "You know I'm a scientist. I'm not calling anyone a liar, and I'm not even saying the map is a fake. I'm just saying the odds of finding a lost treasure on a remote island in the middle of nowhere are pretty astronomical. Odds are, even if it's real, that somebody already found the gold a hundred years back. I think the chance of locating something is incredibly small. However, I'm willing to go along for a few more days, if for no other reason than to enjoy some sailing on this great old boat."

"All right, Bones. Let's take a look at the map."

"Here are the ground rules, boys. I'm going to show it to you live. You can't take no pictures of it, and I ain't going to let you study it. You take a quick look and your only task is to see if it looks real."

We were expecting a crumpled up almost indecipherable piece of parchment paper, something that would fall apart when we touched it. Someone was smarter than to hope it would hold together long enough to find the treasure. It was completely encased in a block of resin. It was plainly readable and would never disintegrate more than the state it had been in when it was preserved.

"Alright fellas. You've had your look. What do you think?"

"It certainly looks old and since I don't read Spanish, I would never be able to follow it anyway. Bones, here's what I think. You've been good to us. You weren't lying about the *Dark Lady* and I don't have any reason to not trust you now. I'm in for at least a while. How long will it take to get to the Turneffe Island?"

"The Turneffe is more than one island. It's a number of islands off the coast. Where we're headed is just one smaller speck of land off the coast. It's called Ambergris Caye. One side of it's got folks living on it. The other, where we'll be going, is still jungle. If this wind holds, two days and we're there. On day three, we should have a truckload of gold onboard. What do you say? Tom" David?"

"We're enjoying the sailing. We'll go."

David noted that Tom worked for himself.

"Tom won't fire himself, but I may need to hire on to *Dark Lady* full time if I'm a week late getting back to my boss. Hell, I hate that job anyway."

"Boys. We have a mission. What about the girls?"

"Trust me, they're good for two more weeks instead of leaving them in Mexico. We'll cut them in for one share between them if they stay with us. If there's as much gold as you say there is, everybody will have more than enough to retire in style."

"There is, boys, there is. Old Bones will never lead you astray. You stick with old Bones."

He took another long draw from his pipe and walked back to the wheel. He put his arm over Triste's shoulders and remarked to him, "Great job on the wheel, matey. You're going to be a first class sailor."

Triste beamed from ear to ear. "Señor Bones, you are certainly the finest captain anywhere."

Bones nodded in agreement. "You're right, matey. I am."

Dark Lady continued on, parting the dark blue water as night fell over the Gulf, and we all collapsed into our bunks until it was our turn to take over the wheel or be on watch.

7

At least two crew always remained on deck while we were under sail. One manned the wheel and the other maintained a watch to make certain no other vessel was on a course that could intersect with ours. A collision at sea never has a happy ending. By now it was hard to tell if we were all insane, or just four guys more than a little disillusioned by our lives, grasping for something in the way of adventure, no matter how ridiculous it seemed. Nonetheless, we were on an old wooden schooner, off the coast of Mexico, headed to a distant tropical island to find a pot of gold.

By morning, our ship was making eight knots under shortened sail. The wind had picked up considerably overnight. As I was falling asleep, I heard the howling begin as the wind started to sing through the rigging. Every sailor worth his salt can tell when the weather is changing, even in the middle of a deep sleep.

At dawn I awoke to find Susanne and an almost fully recovered Karen in the galley making scrambled eggs for the crew. The smell of fresh coffee permeated the air below and merely getting a whiff of it shook the cobwebs out of my head. Strangely, I found it refreshing to hear women laughing and talking in the cabin. I walked over to the galley and asked Susanne if I could have a cup.

"You sure can, Hawkins. Here, I'll get one for you."

"It's not Hawkins. My real name is Jim Hardison. Bones likes to call everyone by a nickname. He stuck me with Hawkins, a character in a novel."

"Sure, little Jim Hawkins in Treasure Island! I don't think you look much like a ten-year-old, though."

"Me neither."

"Does Bones have some sort of fantasy thing going about pirates and treasure?"

"You have no idea. Let me get a swallow of coffee, and I'll update you on the latest. You and Karen are already on a treasure hunt. It's most likely a wild goose chase, an old man's flight through the world of delusion, or perhaps we've all gone mad."

"What are you talking about?"

"You ladies keep cooking. I'll tell you all about it and keep you entertained as you work."

I pressed my nose over the cup and breathed in the delicious aroma. I always thought the smell of coffee was at least half of the enjoyment of a good cup. Seeing the steam come off the almost full cup, I carefully sipped a small sample. "God, this coffee tastes good."

Over the next thirty minutes, I told the ladies of the previous evening's revelations. They didn't protest the absurdity of it at all. They seemed genuinely enthused at the prospects of adventure, whether it resulted in pirate's gold or just a great trip on a schooner. After I finished my eggs and third cup of coffee, I went topside to find Tom at the wheel. Bones and Triste were below in their bunks after a long night of steering *Dark Lady* through the growing seas. Tuna and Dave were securing everything on deck; they too realized the weather was deteriorating. Tuna came over to Tom and me.

"Guys, I'm a little nervous about the weather. Without a radio or a GPS, we don't know exactly what our position is. Yes, Bones knows the general direction we're heading, but there's no way he could know within fifty miles our exact location. The weather could turn ugly and we'd be caught in it with no way of knowing what to expect. Trust me, it can get very ugly out here."

"I know. There's not much difference between the Gulf of Mexico, the Caribbean Sea, or the Atlantic Ocean. If the weather gets severe, it's dangerous out here. Let's just secure everything as if we expect the worst. Never hurts to be cautious."

"I'm with you. Let's shorten sail and rig for heavy weather."

Our cautious approach was all too soon proving to be the correct one. The wind was increasing dramatically and by noon, we were in nothing less than a tropical storm. With no instruments, we could only estimate the wind speed, and we all guessed about the same high number. Tom was struggling with the wheel and with his six foot six frame and two hundred fifty pounds plus, it had to be difficult steering if it was working him that hard. As the wind continued to grow in intensity, the wave heights began to climb. David broke out the life vests and everyone topside grabbed one and put it on. David was smiling as he tightened the straps on his jacket.

"We wanted adventure. Well, my good friends, here is adventure. It's hitting us right in the face. *Dark Lady* seems to handle the waves just fine. I'd say we've got some fifteen footers off our port, stern quarter right now. What do you think about our sails? Should we shorten them again? With all the rigging being manual, it's a hell of a lot easier to do it now than when the wind is even higher."

I had been in some pretty strong nor'easters in the Gulf Stream off the southeastern coast of the U.S., so I knew how bad it could get. "My vote is to run under just a staysail. We can take the foresail down completely and put up a storm sail. With winds this high, we don't need to put any more strain on the sticks than we have to. I'll help you do it."

Over the next thirty minutes, we struggled in the high winds to balance out the sails and tried to keep enough sail up to hold steerage in front of the seas, which were starting to get very nasty looking. Susanne came up from below and walked over to me. "Oh my gosh! Do I need to start getting scared yet?"

"It's hard to tell. No radio; no electronics of any kind. This could be anything from just a late summer storm to a hurricane. We don't have a clue. I'm pretty sure it's nothing that's going to go away soon. See the pattern in the sky? That's called a mackerel sky and you don't see that unless there's severe weather coming. If you're going to stay up here, you need to get a life jacket on."

"Okay, I'm scared."

"I think 'concerned' is a better word. I know this old boat is built strong and the guys sailing her have been sailing a long time. Granted, we sail a lot smaller boats than this, but it's similar in many ways. I think we'll be fine. I just wish we knew where the hell we were."

"You don't know where we are?"

"Like I said, no electronics. We have an idea where we are, but that's about it. We'll be keeping a sharp watch out for other ships and, of course, on our starboard side, we'll look for any sight of land."

"Good grief. Please don't tell any of this to Karen. She's just getting over being seasick and this will put her down again; count on it."

I found her instinct to joke about the situation, rather than sit in a corner and cry, very attractive, but there was very little about

Susanne I didn't find attractive. For the moment, there was a lot more to consider than what turned me on though.

Over the next two hours, the sky darkened and the wind reached what had to be hurricane strength. The waves coming up behind us looked like a mountain chain. They would race up to our stern and just when it looked like they would crash right over top of us, *Dark Lady* would rise up on top of them pushing her stern almost straight up and then she would slide down the face of the wave for what seemed like an hour until the wave ran under us. Tom was tiring at the wheel. I could see the strain in his face.

"How are you doing, Tom?"

"Somebody needs to spell me. I've about had it. The boat seems to be under control with the sails we have up. If they don't split out, she's riding about as good as you could hope for."

"I'll take a turn at it. Susanne, you want to help me at the wheel?"

"Sure, I'll give you moral support. I don't believe I could turn that wheel if I had to."

"Moral support will be fine."

I took the wheel from Tom and could immediately tell why he was drained. Every time *Dark Lady* started to slide down the wave, the tension on the wheel was tremendous. The rudder on a ship this size had to be as big as the side of a barn, and to turn it with just some gears and cables was a struggle. A more modern boat this size would undoubtedly have hydraulic steering. The way a sailboat rides up and down the seas depends on how you turn the wheel. There is a rhythm to steering a sailboat in big seas, and once you get the cadence right, it sort of feels like you're conducting an orchestra. Even in these severe conditions, *Dark Lady* was under control.

More than ever, we were becoming convinced we were caught in a hurricane. It just didn't let up. Wind gusts had to be over a hundred knots. We couldn't hear the person shouting beside us due to the wind and wave noise. I never wanted to test myself to this extreme, but this time, Mother Nature didn't ask me what I wanted. We were here and, for better or worse, we would have to grit it out. Susanne was standing alongside me, and every time a wave hit *Dark Lady*, she would lurch and grab hold of my arm for balance. I anxiously awaited each wave.

In the midst of this surreal scene came a sight straight out of a B movie. The door to the companionway opened up and out stepped Bones. He was singing an old sea ditty and holding a half empty bottle of rum by the neck. Triste was just behind him, and he came over to me, and pleaded with me to send Bones back below. "Señor Jim. Captain Bones is very drunk. He should not be up here. He'll fall in the ocean and drown. Please stop him."

"Okay, Triste, but you go below and find Karen. I want you to look out for her, and I'll watch out for Bones."

"You promise?"

"You can count on it, Triste. Now go on below. It's not safe up here unless you're tied on."

Bones grabbed a stanchion for support, looked at the hell all around us, and smiled. He took a large swallow from the bottle and pushed the cork back in the top. He continued singing as he walked over to where I was standing at the wheel. He slapped me on the back and screamed over the roaring wind, "Beautiful, eh Hawkins? Don't worry. *Dark Lady*'s done this a lot of times over the years. She's not even groaning down below yet. When it gets really ugly, she starts moaning a little. I think she enjoys these little blows." Bones continued stumbling around the deck, periodically singing another verse, taking another swallow, and visiting each member of our little crew, one at a time.

Susanne looked at me. "Is Bones crazy?"

"I'm not sure. He's certainly straight out of a novel, that's for sure. I hope he's not just leading us all to a watery grave."

It was about this time that the companionway door opened yet again. This time, Karen came out with panic painted on her face. "We're sinking! There's water coming in below. It's above the floor in my cabin."

That was not what I needed to hear right then. I called to Tom and David. They cautiously stumbled back to the wheel.

"Guys, Karen says there's a lot of water coming in below. You need to take Susanne and Bones with you, at least what's left of him. He's drunker than hell. Try to get him to go below, and see if you can find out where the water's coming from. Wonder why the bilge pump didn't keep up with it?"

Tuna reminded me. "It's electronic, remember?"

"That explains that. Maybe there's a manual pump."

"We'll check it out. You got it up here?"

"I think so. Go find where the water's coming from."

Bones waved them off as they tried to get him below. He continued his drunken march on deck, bottle still in hand.

Now growing very apprehensive, I fought with the wheel to keep the boat running down the face of a huge wave, much like a surfboard. Each time the hull bottomed out in the valley at the base of the wave trough, the bow would bite down into the ocean to the point that the sides of the bow were under water almost to the top rail – normally the rail would be over ten feet off the water. Most sailors have read with keen interest, accounts of severe weather at sea and wondered how well they would handle it. Would they panic? Would they get so seasick that they couldn't operate the vessel? That's the case with most of the people the Coast Guard has to remove from boats during severe weather. After the Fastnet race off the coast of Britain back in 1979, the approaches to handling a sailboat in extreme weather all changed. Prior to then, the generally accepted approach was to heave to, or depower the boat enough that it would basically sit still and keep its bow into the waves. In most storms, that would work, but in extreme weather like we were having, that opened up the possibility of pitch poling, or flipping lengthwise, bow over stern. Also, the waves could be so tall and close together that the hull might bridge two wave crests, and with no support under the middle of the ship, simply break in two. Quite a number of sailboats in the Fastnet heaved to and sank. Twenty-three boats were sunk or disabled and fifteen lives were lost. After that it was determined the best approach is to continue sailing the boat and keep the waves behind the boat. So far, *Dark Lady* was responding to that method and our shortened sail was proving to be the correct balance for maintaining steerage.

The two immediate concerns were the water coming in below and an inebriated Bones walking around on deck, taking swigs from the rum bottle and singing. He saw that I was watching him with concern and moved over beside me. "It's the curse, Hawkins. The damned curse."

"What curse?"

"The Spaniards stole all the gold from the Mayans; you know the story. They killed their priests and tons of natives. They looted their temples and were hauling it home to Spain to help them fund a bunch of wars they were fighting. The Mayan priests cursed them and the gold. The curse has been going on for almost four hundred years."

"Bones, you're too smart to believe that crap."

"Look at the facts, my friend. There were twenty-eight boats in the Spanish fleet. Twenty-eight, mind you. All disappeared. Just a couple folks left to tell the tale. Mel finds some of the fleet and grabs the gold. The federal government went after him and then the state of Florida. Had to fight over a hundred court claims on the gold. Then, worst of all, his son and daughter-in-law died in a storm one night as they were guarding the wreck. Mel ended up broke even after finding over a billion in gold."

"If you believe all this, why do you want to risk it?"

"I'm already a dead man. Used up my nine lives years ago, most of them in 'Nam. I'm willing to risk it all if it means just having one full year of doing exactly what old Bones wants to do. I'm just like everybody else. Captain Bones wants to feel rich at least once in his life. Now, are you still on 'go' to help me?"

"I don't believe in curses, Bones. This is just a bad storm, a really bad storm."

"Where's the rest of the boys?"

"Water is coming in down below. They're trying to find the source."

"It's always the same source. I'll go show 'em what to do."

Bones disappeared below. I initially thought it was best if he didn't go below in his present state while they were all trying to fix things, but if he knew what the problem was, then he needed to go below and help them find whatever was taking on water. About thirty long minutes later, a greasy group of guys came topside. Tom explained the problem.

"It's fixed. We'd have never found it. Bones came down, and geez, is he smashed. Anyway, he went straight to it. The rudderpost leaks around it like a sieve in these huge following seas. We took half a bed sheet, cut it into ribbons and packed it inside the sleeve around the rudderpost. It's still dripping some, but not enough to hurt anything. Then we had to use a manual pump in the engine room to pump the water out. I think we're all right now. What's the situation out here?"

"Biggest seas I've ever seen; wind probably steady at eighty-five knots, gusting to over a hundred. This old boat is stronger than hell. I don't think the storm is getting any worse. If everything holds together, we'll probably make it. That is if the Mayan curse doesn't jump on us like Bones said it would."

"Oh yeah, what's that all about? He was stammering on about it when he came below."

"I'll tell you later. Where's Bones now?"

"He's passed out in his bunk. We pulled out his lee cloth to keep him from being dumped on the floor and breaking his neck. He's in the right place, sleeping it off."

"Good. And what about the ladies?"

"Karen's back in her bunk. She had just gotten well when this hit. She's chumming again. I doubt she'll ever go on another cruise as long as she lives after this experience."

"And Susanne?"

"She's a real trooper. She and the kid cleaned up the mess where Karen heaved her guts out, and now she's mopping up the rest of the water so everything below doesn't get any more drenched than it already is; a good kid and a really neat lady."

"Tell me about it. Are you up to spelling me at the wheel a few minutes? My arms are starting to cramp up."

"No problem. Why don't you go below and dry off for a little while?"

"Great idea."

I went below and immediately saw Susanne and Triste still busy trying to secure everything. We had thought we were ready for a storm, but the violent motions that *Dark Lady* was experiencing had dumped almost everything that wasn't nailed down into the middle of the floor. I walked over to her. "You okay, Susanne?"

"Better than I thought I would be, thanks to Triste helping me with the nasty work. It's hard not to get a little disoriented down here with all the rolling we're doing. But I'm no worse for wear."

"I'm very impressed. Most people couldn't stay down here and not feel sick. You've got a natural ability to deal with the motion. You'll make a great sailor. Can I help you with anything? I've got a little time before I have to go back to the wheel and relieve Tom and David."

"Let me ask you a question."

"Ask away."

"What's your full name and are you married?"

I was floored by the directness of her question.

"I'm James Robert Hardison and I'm divorced. I've been single for about five years."

Since she asked me first, I thought I'd answer the question she didn't ask. "There's no lady in my life other than my boat, *Last Dance*. How about you? What's your situation?"

"Single, divorced also. I'm a teacher by necessity, but I've always thought I had been dropped off by gypsies, not the stork. I've got wanderlust to spare. I kinda like being out here on the ocean in a sailboat."

"If this storm and your problems in Mexico didn't scare you off, you must have the soul of an adventurer. We'll have to talk some more when, and if, we survive this storm."

"I'll look forward to it, Jim."

I had to admit it. I was smiling large when I returned topside. Triste walked up behind me while I was putting my life vest back on. "You like her, don't you, Señor Jim?"

"What makes you think that?"

"She thinks that. She told me so while we were working down here."

"Really? What did she say?"

"She said she thought you were a very nice guy, the kind a woman would want in their life and the kind she said she never had. So, I think you will do very well with her. Do you like her also?"

"Well Triste, my very observant friend, let's say she's the kind of woman any man would want in their life. I'll leave it at that. Now, you try and get some sleep. We'll need some fresh help up here in the morning to get the boat straight."

"Yes, sir."

I admit I was very attracted to Susanne. I was also quite excited to think she might be interested in me as well. I was ready to continue my turn at the wheel.

"I'm back. The cramps in my arms have eased off. You might want to go get cleaned up a little too. You are covered in grease from the engine room."

"That's my plan. You see this handle beside the wheel?"

"Yes. What's that for?"

"It's got a line going through the pedestal, down through the deck to the main salon. It rings that large brass bell that you see next to the doorway leading aft. You have any problems while we're cleaning up, you yank on that handle and we'll run right back up."

"Got it. I'll be fine." I didn't believe it was getting any worse. The wind would come and go in spurts. *Dark Lady* was handling it far better than I would have ever dreamed possible. Right now it was a matter of waiting for the storm to pass. It couldn't last more than another five or six hours, even if it was a hurricane. They normally move at a pretty fast clip and if you can hang on, you'll eventually get clear. The motion was steady. I wanted to spell the guys for as long as I could stand it, so I would move the steering wheel in concert with the waves to keep the boat on a steady heading. This meant applying a good deal of strength at just the right moment before a wave could strike the hull with enough force to alter the course. It was during one of these hard maneuvers that a loud crack pierced the sound of the wind. It coincided with the wheel I had so firmly grasped, starting to spin freely in my hands. I knew immediately it could mean only one thing, and it had happened at the worst possible moment in time. I grabbed the bell handle and yanked on it about ten times. Within seconds Tuna appeared at the companionway.

"What's the problem?"

"We've lost steering. The rudder cable must have snapped. I heard it pop just when the wheel lost tension. We can't stay like this very long or we'll quickly be broadside to the seas and broach. Get everyone and check out the cable connections."

"All right. We're on it. We know right where the rudderpost is since we just finished packing it with the sheet. We'll start there."

"Make it superfast."

Dark Lady was already starting to respond to the waves. If we couldn't get it stabilized and we broached, it could mean the end of *Dark Lady* and probably all of us as well. The guys, who had just gotten on clean, dry clothes after their work stopping the rudderpost leak, were heading back into the bowels of the ship to locate the snapped cable. Tom held a battery-powered spotlight; David carried a tool bag; and our resident mechanical genius Tuna led the search for the problem. He had concerns that I had not thought of.

"Let's hope it's just the cable and not a broken rudder post or the capstan where the cables connect. A cable break we could probably fix with a section of cable and two clamps."

As they neared the rudderpost, the rolling of the boat became extreme. They all knew what that meant. David said it first, "We're broadside to the waves. We're dead in the water and we've got to get this fixed quick! What's that slamming noise?"

Tom shined the spot onto the now-visible rudderpost. Tuna surveyed the situation, "The cable has snapped in two between the first two blocks on the port side. Shine the spot over there, Tom. Right there. We've got to do something fast. The rudder is swinging wildly and if it breaks loose from the post, we'll truly have no steerage at all and that would be disastrous. Have we got any cable? I think we need about three or four feet and two clamps. I don't know how we can stretch it tight enough to actually steer the boat the way the rudder is swinging and pulling it. The loose end of the cable could cut you in half if it hits you. I hope we can grab the cable and hold it long enough to clamp it back together."

David found a piece of chain in a wooden parts box in the corner of the engine room.

"Guys, how about this? It's a come-along with a chain. We can use it to pull the rudder to one side and tighten it up so we can heave to 'til after the storm has passed."

"That's the best idea I've heard. Let's secure one end to the capstan on the top of the rudderpost and the other to the framing on the starboard side."

Once the device was connected to the rudder and the hull, Tom cranked the come-along handle and pulled the chain tight. Tuna went topside and relayed the plan, "Jim, here's what you need to do. We've secured the rudder hard to starboard. We need to forget about the wheel and back the jib over to force the boat to heave to."

With the boat hove to, the rudder was forcing the bow into the wind and the jib was pulled over to the side of the hull that was closest to the direction the wind was blowing from. In effect, they worked against each other and kept the boat almost stationary with the bow pointing into the wind. It was the tactic advised against for extremely severe weather after the Fastnet Race but, for now, it was the only possible course of action. It would certainly be better than lying a-hull, broadside to the huge waves that were breaking all around us. The crew strained against the hurricane force winds to back the sail over. After fifteen minutes of herculean effort, they succeeded in the maneuver and *Dark Lady* slowly turned into the wind and waves. Even though the seas were a raging maelstrom all around, the great old schooner seemed to breathe deep and settle-in to wait out what could only be considered a hurricane.

Mistakenly we thought the worst was over. At eight that evening, just when we were watching for any kind of break in the storm, we heard a roar above all the din we were already experiencing. It caught all of our attention. I looked over at the boys. "What the hell is that?"

Tom offered his opinion, "I'm certain there are no railroad tracks out here, and I always heard that tornados sound like trains. It's either a waterspout or we have a train somewhere near us."

The noise drew closer and closer. It was already so dark that there was no way to get any bearings on what was approaching other than by the sound it was generating. The sound grew closer. Within two minutes, we were engulfed by a blast of wind and water at least double what we had already experienced.

"Hang on to something. It's a waterspout! Get low on the deck and grab onto anything solid. I could hear the ripping of our headsail as it blew it out like a candle on a ten-year-old's birthday cake. Then the unmistakable sound of a timber cracking. Either the bowsprit or the topmast had cracked before the sail gave out. If it was the topmast, we were all very lucky the sail blew out. Having that large wooden spar fall onto the deck and us, sixty feet below could be disastrous. There was no need to yell anything else to anyone as the noise was deafening. Wind-driven water was actually moving horizontally with the ocean, and it drilled into our faces like water bullets. It was impossible to even keep our eyes open.

The real danger was getting impaled by a wind-blown piece of debris. Anything lying loose on the deck, no matter how small, became a projectile. I knelt down behind the wheel and tried to use it like a shield. The spout practically lifted *Dark Lady* out of the sea and spun her. It seemed to last hours, when in reality, it only lasted seconds. It was very fortunate for us that we had secured everything on deck when the storm had first approached. Anything left topside would have been history. As quickly as it came, it passed. I immediately called out each crewmember's name and was relieved to find that all of us were still onboard and intact. I'll never live long enough to forget the sound of that waterspout as it went over top of us.

For the next five hours, the storm blew unabated. Numerous lines and items secured topside either snapped in two or broke free. Thankfully, none of these losses were of the same life-threatening caliber as the rudder cable failure.

As midnight approached, the wind started to subside. Accordingly, the waves took their cue and reduced in size. Our crew, now all gathered on deck, breathed a collective sigh of relief. I'm certain that for years to come, all of us will tell and retell the account of riding out a hurricane in the Caribbean aboard the *Dark Lady*. It is a tale that will require no exaggeration to make it more exciting. Like the rest of the crew, I was just glad to have survived the ordeal. We continued to ride hove-to, well after sunrise, as we all slept in, totally exhausted.

By noon, Tuna and David were below removing the come-along from the rudder and using it to pull the two loose ends of the broken cable together and put in a splice using the chain on the come-along. It wasn't the ideal fix, but it was workable, at least until we could make it to a port. Deciding where to put into port would now be a priority. We were all more than a little concerned about landing in any place in Mexico, but it might not be feasible with *Dark Lady*'s problems to go any farther south without needed repairs being made. Running into another strong storm without permanent repairs in place would be extremely risky. By 4:00 p.m., the seas were small and the wind was a comfortable fifteen knots. We were making good time heading south.

8

Bones called for a crew meeting at dinner that evening. We left David at the wheel while everyone else met in the main salon over the great meal Susanne and a nearly-recovered Karen had prepared to celebrate our still being alive to eat. Bones addressed the crew. "Boys, I think first of all, we should thank these wonderful ladies for making this great meal for us. I know I'm ready for some good chow, and they cook a helluva lot better than any of us can. Thank you, Susanne and Karen."

We all raised our glasses and in unison shouted, "Here! Here!"

Bones then proceeded, "And let's not forget the contributions of the youngest member of our crew. Triste here stayed below and helped Susanne when it was awful down here. He's a strong-willed lad, he is. Here's to Triste."

The youth was flattered and proud to be recognized. Praise was something his life had been sorely lacking. I didn't know what lay in store for him, but it had to be better than what he came from.

Bones was in a gregarious mood. "Gentlemen and ladies, we have been tested mightily these past two days and came through with flying colors. I'm proud as punch of all of you. I could feel it when I met you that you was all special. Now I know that feeling was right. Anyway, we all know we need to put in somewhere that has marine facilities to do a proper repair on *Dark Lady*. I think we can clear Mexico and pull in just past their border with Belize. We can do our repairs there and take on a few supplies. I know for sure that we need a little more rum. Oh, and I do apologize if I partook a little too much yesterday. I kinda got caught up in the moment.

"As far as my talking out of turn about the Mayan curse and all, well, that's just an old wives' tale. Sailors love to pass on those sorts of stories to folks. Don't know why exactly, but we obviously get some sort of kick out of it. I apologize if I scared you with that nonsense. Now, are we all together on sailing into Belize?"

Tuna was still skeptical of Bones' ability to know just where we were. "Bones, how far away from Belize are we, and what course heading would we have to take to get there? How long will it take?"

"Boys, we can be there morning after next. We'll head about 185 degrees southwest, and I think that will take us straight there."

"How do you know that?"

"I'm the captain and I'm really good at what I do."

"God, I hope so."

"It's a done deal. We're heading for Belize."

After the meal, I walked up on deck to enjoy the peaceful night. As I made my way forward, I noticed Susanne standing against the rail looking out to sea. After the financial ruin I had experienced with the collapse of my first marriage, I was extremely hesitant about allowing myself to get involved romantically with another woman. For some reason, I was throwing all of those concerns aside to find out more about her.

"Beautiful out here, isn't it?"

"Oh hi, Jim. Yes, this is much more than I could have imagined. Even with the hurricane hitting us, I'm still glad I'm here."

"I am too. Though there's definitely some danger involved, at least I feel like I'm actually living and experiencing things. I don't know how I ever spent so many years in a cube farm staring at a computer screen, pretending I was remotely interested in what I was doing. I hated every second I was there, but I stayed."

"Why? Why didn't you just leave?"

"My wife, family, kids, responsibilities. I guess that's the excuse I want to use. My ex considered any life other than putting in a forty-hour week an aberration of the American dream. She was terrified of any sort of change or risk. If I had it all to do over again, I wouldn't. I know that for sure. I stayed because I didn't want my kids growing up in a broken home. I stayed until they were out of high school and away at college. I hope they benefited from my staying, but I'm not sure if it hurt them more than it helped. They knew their parents weren't happy with each other. There was always arguing and had hard feelings. Actually, I tried not to participate in the fussing. I can't stand arguing. That only made my ex angrier. She lived to fight. She was Erma Bombeck's answer to professional wrestling. She could have been called the Incredible Mad Housewife. The lightweight belt would have been hers. No man could stand against her."

"Surely, you're exaggerating."

"Well, maybe some, but not much. Why did you get divorced?"

"Much simpler. My husband decided he wanted to run away with his secretary. She was barely twenty and had the IQ of a field mouse. For him, that was perfect. They're not together anymore, but hey, he had his fling. Cost him a home and a faithful wife. Not that either meant anything to him."

"Has that discouraged you from, well, thinking about another man?"

"It certainly affects the kind of man that I'd look for. I know all the qualities I don't want in one."

The breeze was blowing through Susanne's dark, curly hair and brushing it onto her shoulders against her olive skin. She had a fresh smell that blew my way and filled me with a desire for her unlike any I had ever experienced. She smiled as she talked, and it seemed to me that someone had taken every detail of a woman that I found attractive and combined it all in this one perfect creature. I was lost completely in the moment and was not totally in control of my sanity when I bent toward her and kissed her squarely on the lips as she talked. She was undoubtedly surprised and would probably have told me to stop if I didn't have her lovely lips firmly under the embrace of mine. Instead of resisting, I felt her grow soft and pliable throughout her entire being. She slowly reached behind my neck and gently stroked it. She returned my passion as if she had been waiting for this exact same moment all her life. The sexual heat between us was building with runaway intensity. I pulled her close against me and our full body press left no doubt in either of our minds what we both wanted. I backed off after a full two minutes of passionate embrace.

"Please forgive me for being so aggressive. I don't know what came over me. I never do anything like this. At least not before this."

"You don't have to apologize or explain. I'm feeling just what you're feeling."

"What should we do? I mean we barely know each other."

Without hesitation, she looked me squarely in the eyes a slight smile on her lips. "I know all I need to know. I think it would be completely appropriate for us to go below to my bunk, pull the door shut to the cabin and make love all night."

"That's amazing. You read my mind completely."

We both tried to act nonchalant as we walked the length of the deck, not touching or holding hands, but almost touching our sides as we headed toward the companionway. As we walked past the wheel, Bones and Triste, standing side by side steering *Dark Lady*, watched us with interest.

As we neared the steps to go below, Bones called out, "Have a lovely evening, you two."

I looked at Susanne who was smiling. "Must be pretty obvious, eh?"

"I think it's written all over our faces."

We shut the door to the small crew cabin that Susanne had been using and immediately started back where we had left off on deck. I had never experienced such a flood of passion in my life. This was not just sex. It was something so beyond that it approached the spiritual. It was primal; something that nature placed into man to see that we chose a woman and continued the species. At this moment, I wanted this woman more than I had wanted anything in my life. I didn't want to rush anything about this incredible experience. Unfortunately, the part of me that was animal wanted to rip all the clothes off this exciting and alluring woman and breed with her immediately. Somewhere between those two desires, I found myself and we undressed each other while exploring each other's bodies for the first time. I knew Susanne was trim and fit, but her body showed a woman who was athletic and more than just desirable. She was, for me, the perfect definition of beauty. I was not looking for a woman with every feature perfect and no wrinkles to be found. I found a face with a few traces of experience around the edges very intriguing. The wrinkles on Susanne's face came from the best kind of wrinkles possible, smiling. She exuded warmth, kindness, intelligence and desirability, all the ingredients I sought in a woman. It would be hard to restrain myself around her from here on out. I probably wouldn't even try. We spent most of the night releasing the tensions created by years of unsatisfied needs and emotional frustrations. I knew I would do whatever it took to nurture and cement this relationship.

After we were fully sated, we stayed awake and talked for hours. We had just fallen into a deep sleep when the first rays of sunlight broke through the porthole that illuminated the tiny cabin. We were snuggled as close as two separate bodies could be when Triste knocked on the door. "Señor Jim, I hate to wake you, but Captain Bones says you are needed on deck. Good morning, Susanne."

"Good morning to you, Triste. We'll be up in just a minute."

I looked over at this strikingly beautiful woman. Her dark hair was now uncombed and falling naturally over her shoulders. Her firm physique was feminized each time she moved, and her spectacular breasts undulated with every movement of her body. Just watching her was throwing gasoline back on my fire. I was the first to make the suggestion.

"No one will hate us if we are just a little longer going topside, will they?"

"They would have to be terribly mean-spirited to be upset at all, in my opinion. I say we go for it."

Another hour of heaven peeled off the master timepiece of life while we savored each other once more. I was getting to the point that if we could have room service deliver food to us, I would stay in bed with her for the next month. I had had no idea how unbelievable sex could be, until this. I had never believed in love at first sight, but I had been wrong.

Pulling ourselves apart was difficult, but we managed to straighten ourselves up enough to be presentable to others, and headed up the companionway to go topside. Bones, with his ever present shadow, Triste, was once again manning the wheel. David, Tom, Tuna, and Karen were also up early, straightening up the deck after the beating everything took from the hurricane. Bones saw us and started in with the jawing I knew was certain to come, "Good morning, darlings. I trust you got your beauty rest last night? I seriously doubt it. Sounded to me like the boys were down below working the manual bilge pump again. Boom, boom, boom, all night long."

He soon had the crew in stitches at our expense. It was a price I didn't mind paying at all.

"Okay, Admiral Bones. What do you want me to do this morning?"

"You could take the wheel if you would be so kind. I need to get a second, third, whatever, cup of joe this morning. Miss Karen, even though still weak from her bout with *mal de mer*, rose quite early and fixed a delicious breakfast. I, of course, was unable to join the rest of the crew at the table, since I had no one to spell me on the wheel. But, what price, love? Am I right?"

"Go get your coffee, Bones. You can't hurt my feelings. You just wish someone as lovely as Susanne found your scraggly, old presence, of interest."

"I've had plenty of admirers for your information. Not that it's important. Lots of women find men like me attractive. You know, powerful men who are an authority figure."

"Go get your coffee, Bones. You're disturbing me with those visuals. I got the wheel."

Susanne was unfazed by the kidding as well, "Bones, I ain't one of those women. You're cute in an elfish sort of way, but definitely not my type."

"What you don't know is your loss, sweetheart. Anyway, I'm glad you lovebirds are up and about. Nothing wrong with love, my friends. Nothing at all."

Bones and Triste disappeared below. It was interesting to see the dynamics between them. "I think Triste has a real interest in the sea and sailing. Strangely enough, he admires Bones for God knows what reason."

"Bones has his own unique qualities. On a boat like this, I think his talents have their place. I'm going to go below and help Karen clean up after breakfast. You embarrassed to kiss me with everyone looking?"

I gave her my answer by bending over, left hand on the wheel and right arm around her shoulders and giving her a kiss on the lips any woman would be proud to tell their girlfriends about. She returned the favor, smiled, and went below. Tom and David gave me the thumbs up sign as she walked away. No need to keep our attraction to each other a secret. We couldn't hide it if we wanted to.

Susanne and Jim

Bones came back on deck after he had finished his third cup of coffee and walked over to me. "Hawkins, keep your eyes open and keep heading west. I'm betting you'll start to see shoreline by four this afternoon. There's some shallow water and reefs around here, so the first change you see in water color, you call me immediately. We'll send somebody up the mast a ways to help us find the deep water."

I still don't understand how Bones could feel where we were. At 4:15 precisely, Tom called out from his perch on the lower spreaders, about thirty-five feet up the foremast, "Land ho, to starboard, ten degrees."

I turned *Dark Lady* accordingly, and we began to run toward shore. When you're on a sailboat, the first sight of land can often be a long time prior to actually arriving. Over the next two hours we slowly and very carefully plodded along, watching all the while for coral heads, which are masses of hardened coral that rise up from the ocean floor to just below the surface of the water. The coral is as hard as concrete and the hull of a boat would be no match for it in the case of a collision. Coral heads have been responsible for a great many wrecks. Fortunately, on a clear day, they aren't hard to see. They're much lighter in color than the surrounding water and from his perch above the deck, Tom was able to see them and call out instructions needed to avoid them. We went in as fast as was prudent, looking for deep water and, hopefully, a channel into some sort of anchorage. By 6:30 p.m. we were tied up to a small commercial dock alongside numerous fishing boats. We ran up the yellow quarantine flag to let the custom's office know we were an out-of-country visitor. It wasn't hard to remember our last experience with the custom's officers in

Mexico. That piece of history was to rejoin us quickly. We had not arrived at our desired destination. We had sailed into the small Mexican village of Xcalak.

Bones studied the remote little port town. "Boys, this ain't Belize. This place is less than ten miles from the border though. As I recall, there ain't no port authority folks here. I say we take down the quarantine flag, get on with our repairs and see can't we get out of here before tomorrow night. This place ain't on anybody's radar, so I think we'll be okay for a while. Old El Dorado's probably got eyes all up and down the coast so we can't take it for granted he won't find out we're here. Let's just do what we got to do pronto and hit the road."

"Bones, the authorities don't know the women are on board, so why would they be looking for us?"

"You're forgetting the two idiots we threw in the water a couple nights back. I'm sure they have sung every song they knew to keep El Dorado from making dog food out of them. Besides, they don't have to be looking for us. They'll just advise him that we're here in case he's interested. They might not put two and two together. Then again, they just might. I don't want to bet against them. Drug gangs in Mexico ain't nobody to go afoul of. There's folks here that would put a bullet in you for a twenty dollar bill. So, let's just play it safe."

On the other side of the small gravel road that ran along the beach, I spotted a quaint little bar. I thought it would be great to have one nice, cold beer ashore before we busted our butts doing the repairs. I saw the other guys checking it out as well. David threw out the question we were all thinking, "Bones, how about just one quick beer across the street? There's nobody there and I'd like to sit at a table that wasn't moving for one hour and have a cold Corona."

Bones saw the eager expressions on all our faces and relented. "Okay, but let's just hold it to one hour. There's no need to push our luck."

"How about the ladies? They might want to come along too."

"That's taking a chance."

"You don't really think anyone in this hole-in-the-wall is looking for them, do you? They probably think they're back in the States already."

"Trust me, they'd know if they were. Those folks are well-connected even in the States. If it involves their business, they'll know. But I don't guess one beer this late would raise any eyebrows. Tell you what, go on over, and Triste and I will stay with the boat. Don't want to leave her unattended out here. A lot of stuff might just walk off if nobody's watching."

Susanne and Karen came bouncing up the companionway. They had both grabbed some old straw hats Bones kept below for shade on blistering hot days. With their hair pulled under the hats and wearing some old shirts and jeans they had borrowed from Bones' immense wardrobe, they would not draw any attention. The cantina was small and dark with a couple of neon beer signs providing almost all the lighting. Other than the guy behind the bar, we were the only customers. I ordered a round of beer for the crew and asked the bartender for some música. He turned up a small boom box behind the counter, and the Latin singer, Luis Miguel's, voice filled the room with a soft ballad. We all relaxed and discovered very quickly that another drink was in order. Tom picked up the next round. The ladies took off their hats and shook their hair straight. Not having their bags on board meant the best grooming they could get done was with a borrowed hairbrush, Dial soap, and water. I was totally enamored with Susanne and made sure my chair was beside hers and as close as I could get it.

My arm eventually found its way over her shoulder and within a few minutes, my hand was gently stroking her thick auburn hair.

The conversation was happy, and we all felt a sense of relief and pride for surviving the hurricane. As we talked, I couldn't help but notice that Tom and Karen were very much preoccupied with each other. Of course, there were also the telltale signs of interest when Karen laughed excessively at Tom's average joke, touching his arm seductively each time she said something to him. There was something going on there. Susanne noticed as well and leaned over to my side as she whispered, "Something about sharing a sea cruise seems to bring all our hormones to the surface."

"It sure did for me."

We laughed and small talked for about half an hour more. Just as we were finishing up what we had decided would be our third and last beer, two guys who looked like commercial fishermen grabbed a table in the far corner of the place. They ordered a couple of cervezas and lit their cigarettes. They were conversing with each other in hushed tones even though they were speaking Spanish. They kept looking our way. I guess we didn't fit the stereotype of the usual cantina patron for the area.

After a short while, the older of the two men came over to our table. "Buenos noches señores y señoritas. I could not help but admire the beautiful sailing ship that entered our harbor this afternoon. Would that be your boat?"

"Well, it's not our boat, but yes, we did come in on it. Why do you ask?"

"We're not used to seeing such a vessel here. You must be having problems, am I right?"

"Yes, you are correct. We got caught in the hurricane that came through the area, and it did some damage to our rigging."

“Well, if you will permit me to promote my services, my name is Perez and I am an incredible woodworker. If it's woodwork you need, I am your man. Now, did these beautiful señoritas make the journey through the storm with you?"

"They did."

"Very courageous. Not many women would be up to such a trip. From where did you leave?"

I was suddenly beginning to feel that this would-be carpenter was asking a lot more questions than were needed to solicit our business. I looked over at the crew and gave them a look to alert them to my suspicions. I then responded to the man, "Well, nice talking with you. We have to turn in early, as we have a very busy day ahead."

"I see. Are you leaving tomorrow?"

"No. I think we'll be here four or five days getting our repairs finished. We better get going. Have a great evening."

Our suspicions were confirmed as we walked out of the place and saw a late model, large black SUV sitting out front.

"They're doing pretty well for poor fishermen, I'd say."

David reaffirmed my thoughts as well. "Good call, Jim. God, is this whole country on the take?"

"It sure seems like it. No wonder all of their people are trying to move to the States."

We made our way quickly back to the boat. Bones and Triste were on deck waiting for us. Bones wasted no time putting out his *I told you so*. "Those fellas approach you?"

"Sure did. Who do you think they were?"

"Friends of El Dorado. No doubt about it. Big black SUV has drug money written all over it. They saw the girls were with you, right?"

"Yes."

"Okay, we're only a short hop to Belize. We'll wait 'til the middle of the night and ease back out of here. With any luck we can be at Ambergris Caye by sunrise. It's about thirty miles off the coast and it's very close to where the *Princesa* bought the farm. All we have to do is get out of Mexican waters and to where there are some other boats and people around. They won't follow us into Belizean waters. They don't own that government, yet. I'm sure they're working on it though. Did you tell them we were leaving soon?"

"Just the opposite. Once we figured out they were quizzing us, I told them we'd be here four or five days."

"Good. Maybe we'll catch them sleeping."

Shortly after one in the morning, Bones fired up the diesel and kept it at an idle. Tom and David walked down the pier and started to untie the lines from the massive cleats that held them secure. David didn't see the intruder walk up behind him. He almost jumped out of his skin when he was asked, "Why such a hurry, Señor? Your friend said you would be here four days. Why did your plans change so quickly?"

David turned to see one of the two men who had been in the bar earlier. This time, he was holding a pistol. "So, old Bones finally found himself a crew, eh? I think you need to retie your lines and tell your Captain Bones to shut down the motor, or things might get ugly very quickly."

The gunman was as surprised as David when he heard footsteps behind him. He turned just in time to see the two-by-four board Tom was swinging crash directly into his face. There was a very loud smack as it struck him squarely. Tom wanted no chance of the gunman having time to fire his weapon or seek retaliation. He dropped like a brick.

"Let's get out of here before his buddy shows up."

"Thanks, Tom. You saved my ass."

"No problem. I enjoyed it."

"Remind me never to piss you off."

"Will do. Now toss these lines onboard."

In seconds, *Dark Lady* was freed from the pilings that held her to the pier. Bones expertly backed her out into the channel. Without running lights, to avoid being seen, the trick now would be to get out of the narrow channel, surrounded by those nasty coral heads, in the dark. Bones maneuvered *Dark Lady* delicately, at barely a knot. If we struck a coral head, the damage would be minimal.

About ten minutes out from the dock and well into the channel, we all heard the loud, long scraping sound and felt the hull of *Dark Lady* rise up slightly. She had kissed the top of a coral head. As we came off of it, everyone breathed a collective sigh of relief.

After an hour, *Dark Lady* broke out of the channel into deep water. I was growing very aware of just how skilled a sailor Bones was. He was a very strange, larger-than-life personality, and he was a lot more complicated than any initial impressions conveyed. I walked over to the wheel to tell him how impressed I was. "Very nicely done, Captain."

"Thanks. I've been in this channel a number of times. I kinda got a feel for it."

"What will we do about the repairs now?"

"While you fellas were drinking and cavorting with the enemy, I found some nice timbers on the dock and stored them on the aft deck. We should be able to make the repairs with the tools we have onboard once we get to a calm anchorage. We're only a few miles from Ambergris Caye. There's a nice, tight anchorage on the backside that only a few folks know about. Tricky channel with no markers. I know it well. We can not only fix up *Dark Lady* there, but it's just a short sail to where we need to start looking for gold. Does that get you excited? Just hearing the word 'gold' does it for me."

By sunrise, we could see the palm studded shoreline of Ambergris Caye ahead. Bones steered away from the marked channel that led into what appeared to be a fairly well established resort island. Beach homes were clearly visible along the shoreline. Just beyond the reef that wrapped around the Caye, Bones kept a tight course to where water depth dropped from twenty feet to hundreds of feet. The contrast in water color was incredible. The deep water was dark, cobalt blue, and the shallow water was sky blue with clear visibility to the bottom. With the sun overhead, finding deep water was not an issue. Leaving at night in an unmarked channel with no lighting whatsoever, as we had done the past evening, would bed a different matter altogether. Compared to that, this was like walking down a city sidewalk.

Ambergris Caye was a good-sized island. On the backside, it was not nearly so developed. Bones found the break in the reef that led to a very small, secluded lagoon. At this point, it became obvious that he had been here a number of times before. Otherwise, there would be no way on earth he could have ever known this break in the reef existed. There were no other boats inside, and it looked and felt like we had just dropped the hook in Bora Bora. The shore was covered with dense underbrush and crowned with many different types of tropical palms. The beach was as white as a new refrigerator, with undisturbed sand as far as I could see. If I was to be stranded on some remote island, and it looked like this one, I think I would be just fine with it.

The anchor bit into the bottom sand in about thirty feet of water. You could look over the side and clearly see the anchor and tell that one of its flukes was completely submerged in the sand. We had a good hold on the bottom. Bones gathered the crew topsides. "Here's the gist of what has to be done: We need to repair *Dark Lady* before we do another thing. We need to be ready to go out to sea at a moment's notice if things get out of control here. We've already pissed off El Dorado and company, so I don't doubt for a moment they're out looking for us by now. We're not that far away from their world down here. Our best hope is that they don't know this anchorage even exists. Not a lot of folks do. We'll keep a very low profile while we're here and stay away from the developed parts of the island. There's not even a road over to this section of the island. There's a big swamp between here and the rest of the place. Actually, it's a jungle. Not the kind of place that any tourists are going to be traipsing through. We can keep off the radar out here. Now, let's get those repairs done."

We worked at a fevered pace the entire day. After the run-in with the thugs in Mexico, we understood that they had not forgotten about us. I don't think they looked at us as any sort of threat, but they certainly didn't want anyone to think they were weak. Killing us was apparently just a matter of pride to them.

There was urgency in our movements that enabled us to get the repairs done just before sundown. Of course, having Tuna, a gifted engineer on board, helped our cause immensely. By dark, we were all tired and hungry.

Susanne and Karen went below to prepare a hot meal so that we could sit down and eat the moment we were done with our work. We cleaned up a little with a quick rinse on our hands and faces and took our places at the large salon table. The warm teak cabin was softly lit by a brass oil lamp that hung over the table and moved slightly with the gentle motions of *Dark Lady,* causing the light to play against the varnished cabin walls. It was one of the most comfortable main salons I'd ever seen.

Here we were, deep in the western Caribbean Sea, aboard a magnificent vessel and, as ridiculous as it sounded, in search of treasure. It was almost too preposterous to conceive. Yet, here we were. Relieved that the ship was back in seaworthy condition and that we were still alive, the conversation turned to Bones' favorite subject, gold. Apparently, the thought was never far from his frontal lobe.

"Fellas, and ladies, I'll tell you what. We find this load of treasure and all of your lives will be changed beyond anything you could imagine in less than a month. Have you given any thought as to what you'd do if you had more money than you could spend in a lifetime even if you were stupid with it?"

Too much money had never been an issue for me, though the lack of it certainly has had its impact on my life. My financial dream had always been to have enough to pay my bills. Nonetheless, I had been pondering the thought of being rich ever since the whole subject of gold had come up.

"I think I know a few things I'd do. I'd get a larger boat and sail off to all the islands in the Caribbean I've never seen, which is most of them." I looked over at Susanne. "Of course, I'd want someone I thought a lot of to go with me. Who wants to be all alone in paradise?"

Susanne looked over at me and smiled, "Any thoughts as to who that special person would be?"

"I think she knows who she is."

Everyone at the table knew who I meant and a toast was raised to Jim and Susanne. It felt good for everyone to know she and I were a lot more than mere friends. "And, after I cruised the islands, I'd probably buy a nice house beside the water, someplace where palm trees grow, and watch the sun go down 'til my last day. How about you, Tom?"

"I know exactly what I'd do. I've always loved art. I'd visit the Getty Museum, the Guggenheim, the Louvre, all the best galleries. I've always wanted to see Michelangelo's *David*, *The Pieta*, so many great works that I never thought it would be possible to see without a lot of time and money. I'd even buy a few Picassos and Monets. Granted, it would take a ton of money."

Karen looked over at Tom. "And what about a woman in your life? Is there someone special you'd like to share your grand adventure with?"

"Yes. I haven't told her yet, but I think she might be interested in a trip around the world looking at museums."

Karen smiled as she boldly said. "I know I would go if I were fortunate enough to be asked by someone like you."

Tom beamed. "What about you, David? You're up."

"I've been thinking about what I want to do with my life, gold or no gold. I've figured out what's important to me, and I'm going after it."

"What's that, David?"

"Collin and Marshall. My twin boys. They're fourteen now and had their world pretty much torn apart when Leigh and I separated. We met in high school and never really knew anybody else, at least as adults. We married while I was in college and started about the business of being adults before we actually were. I think we missed out on a lot of things while doing the things we thought were important but, in reality, weren't. We walked away from our marriage when things got tough. Instead of pulling together, we went our separate ways. It's been a couple of years and neither of us has found anybody else we're interested in being with. It was a big mistake and I'm going to go home and set it right. It hit me when we were in the hurricane. I was thinking about what was important to me that I hadn't done, who would even miss me if I drowned. The answer just slapped me in the face. I already have a treasure. I really don't even want to finish this trip. As soon as I can get on a plane outta here, I'm heading home. I can fix what's wrong in my life and I'm going to."

Another round of toasts went up, this time, congratulating David on his decision to leave as soon as possible.

Bones looked over at Susanne. "What about you girls? What would you do with a ton of money?"

Susanne answered directly. "I can't speak for Karen, but I think everyone has thought about what would happen if they could do whatever they wanted. I would like to go back to school and get a Ph.D. in history. I've always loved history and wanted to stay in college, but didn't have the money. Here I am, ten years later, still working to pay off the college loans I already have. Being poor really sucks. Okay Tuna, you're up."

"Well, I have to say that I'm about as happy right now as I've ever been. I love being onboard this old schooner with a great bunch of folks. I think I'd just keep on doing this if I could do whatever I wanted. I'll tell you who we haven't heard from. Triste, what will you do with your share of Bones' booty?"

"What's booty?"

"Gold, Triste. Lots of it."

"I know what I'd do if I could. I would go back to my village, move my poppa's grave to the mission cemetery, and have him a fine headstone made. He has nothing now but a small wooden cross. You can't even read his name, but I know it is his. Then I would go find my mother and bring her to live with me. I would buy a small house in the United States, go to school and get a good job. I think I would like to be a ship's captain like Captain Bones."

I knew everyone must be feeling it, so I went ahead and said it. "Okay, I feel completely selfish now. How about everyone else?"

There was some coughing and shuffling of feet and then Bones interrupted the awkward silence. "My turn now, mateys. Knowing that the treasure was there just waiting for me to find a way to get at it, I've had a lot longer to think about it than the rest of you. I'm guessing there's at least as much gold in this little trove as there was in the *Atocha*. With a good measure of silver and lots of contraband jewelry, I'm thinking it's about a billion and a half dollars in all. Of course, every city, county, state, federal and world government there is will go after us if they discover what we've found. That said, I think it's better that we keep our good fortune all to ourselves. We don't go out and buy airplanes or a Rolls Royce. We slowly sell off the gold and jewelry as we actually need the money and just live out all of our years in comfort. Wouldn't it be great to just never have to worry about how to pay for anything ever again? Of course, I do want to fly first class as I travel the world. But that and a fifty-room mansion will be my only luxuries."

He'd caught us all off guard with his little charade of living modestly. "Well, mateys, we need to divide up the night watches again, just like when we're at sea. Only, we ain't looking out for bad weather, coral heads, or other ships. We need to keep a watch out for El Dorado's little band of vultures and any other folks that might be able to figure out what we're up to."

Tom asked the obvious. "How would anyone have any clue what we're up to?"

"The subject of treasure is very closely listened to in the Keys. Believe me, everyone who ever knew Mel or any of his crew knows the story of the missing map. My old boss Nathan would hit the bottle now and again, and I heard him telling some barfly at the Buccaneer that he knew where the rest of the Spanish fleet had disappeared. Most just thought he was drunk and spreading a few good tales around. Others paid real close attention. I guarantee you some folks were more than curious when the *Dark Lady* left port. Word of an adventure like this spreads pretty damned quick. Maybe they know what we're up to; maybe they don't. It's just good business to assume we're being watched. So I'll take the first watch and you fellas can divvy up the others. I'll see one of you on deck at 2:00 a.m."

We were tired and feeling comfortable in the salon. A small bottle of rum was being passed around and most everyone took a shot. After a bit of small talk, David made a comment that got everyone's attention, especially after Bones' remarks.

"You know, when the creep on the dock pulled the gun on me and Tom walloped him, he had just said something to me that's got me thinking. He said, 'So Old Bones finally got him a crew.' How did he know Bones and the *Dark Lady*? To me, it points out the fact that he'd been looking for a crew to help him sail. If they knew that, then they probably know damn well what we're here for and I don't think somebody as ruthless as El Dorado is going to just let us sail off into the deep blue sea without trying to keep a watch out for us. I guarantee you they know we're in the area and what we're doing here. We all need to be very careful. I'm going to try to get to the civilized part of Ambergris tomorrow to catch a ferry or small plane over to the mainland. Then my good friends, I'm headed home to my wife and sons to get my life straightened back out. I owe you all for this experience. Trust me, it's been life changing for me."

"Here's to David and family." We all drank a toast and then it got real quiet as we contemplated what we had just heard. We were undoubtedly at some risk on this expedition.

Bones apparently needed no sleep. He was running on adrenalin. He was up until 2:00 a.m. on his watch then again before sunrise. He had the coffee going and was humming his usual sea ditty and scribbling notes on a pad of paper at the salon table.

9

"Morning, Hawkins. Today we hunt for Mayan gold. With any luck, we'll be loaded with treasure and out of here soon."

"Bones, I hope you're right. I'm not betting the farm on it, but you seem awfully certain about it all, so I'll go along and do what I can to help."

Susanne came into the salon. Her dark hair was only half combed and covered a small portion of her face. She pushed it back from her eyes as she entered. God, she was beautiful. We had been sleeping together every night since our first interlude, and I had to admit that my spirits soared every time she walked into the room.

"Morning, Bones. Jim, you handsome thing, you should have gotten me up with you, so I could fix you some coffee."

"You were sleeping too soundly. Today promises to be a long, tiring one."

Tom and David walked in followed closely by Tuna and Triste. Tuna grabbed a mug from the counter and poured a full cup of straight black coffee. "Ah, just the way I like it. I could smell it back in my cabin. Coffee is the elixir of the Gods and the best alarm clock ever invented. So are we about to go treasure hunting?"

David responded, "Not me. I wish you all the very best. My treasure is back at home. Tom said he'd run me around the point in the dinghy and drop me off at the first sign of civilization. I'll find my way home from there."

"You're sure, David?"

"Never been more certain of what I wanted to do. If you guys find the treasure and all get rich, I'll be your gardener. Just treat me kindly."

"We wish you the best, David. I'll see you in a week or so when we get back home."

There was certainly excitement on board. Whether we were all caught up in the fantasies of a madman or had made a rational decision based upon hard evidence, it was anybody's guess at that point. All that aside, there was a new energy in the group.

Tom would ferry us to the beach and then take David around the point and down the other side of the island to find a spot to set him ashore. We would all meet back at the beach inside the lagoon where *Dark Lady* was anchored. Susanne and Karen gave David big hugs and we all wished him the best as he headed back to the real world while we continued following Bones to "Never Never Land."

Tom and David motored along the coast for about four miles – Ambergris Caye was not a huge island. They watched as a small plane began its descent to what must be the island's runway several miles further down the island.

"That's probably where I need to be heading. Looks like a small community ahead. I can see a few folks walking on the beach. That's a good spot to drop me off." As they approached, they saw several very high-end beach cottages nestled back amongst the palms. Ambergris Caye was a truly tropical paradise. The water was calm and Tom ran the dinghy right up onto the beach. David gave Tom a quick, guy's hug and walked up to one of the locals to ask directions. Tom pushed the dinghy out and headed back.

David got directions to a small ferry landing and started walking the two miles needed to get there. He was told it was only a two hour ferry ride back to the mainland of Belize and that he could easily catch a plane back home from there. The road he was walking along was gravel and dotted with potholes. Though beautiful, the Caye was certainly third world at its core.

After thirty minutes of walking, he could see cars pulling into a square, fenced-in parking lot just ahead. In the background, he spotted a small ferry that was pulled up to a dock and there were people boarding and leaving the craft, simultaneously. He walked over to a ramshackle building and asked where the ferry was heading and how much it would cost. It was only a thirty-dollar ticket, and he was told it would take him the shortest route to the mainland. Satisfied with the answers, David bought his ticket and boarded the sixty-five foot vessel for the short trip. He noticed there was a sharp contrast between the passengers. Some appeared to be very affluent, with their matched luggage, Hawaiian beach shirts, and Nikons. Others were wearing hand-me-downs and bore many of the telltale signs of poverty. He had always heard that the Caribbean nations were this way. It was easy to see why there could be resentment toward visiting Americans. We all seemed rich compared to the poor natives. David knew all of these issues were beyond his scope to solve, so he pushed his bag under his seat and sat back to people-watch during the short trip. The constant work and lack of sleep caught up with him, and he started to doze off in his seat. The trip went by quickly, as he wound up sleeping through the largest part of it. His rest was short lived though, as he was rudely awakened by a hand pushing against his shoulder. The ferry had arrived and everyone was disembarking.

"Sir, wake up, sir. You must come with us, sir."

David opened his eyes to see two men, dressed in casual street clothes, standing directly in front of him. They were not pleasant looking and their expressions were not those of someone on vacation. Each of them appeared to be in a foul mood.

"Who… Who are you? What do you want?"

"You need to come with us, sir. Now."

"What for? I've got a plane to catch. I'm heading back to the States."

"We are with the Belize government, sir. We are custom agents, and we have been asked to question you. We will not do it onboard the ferry, as we don't wish to inconvenience everyone else on board. Grab your luggage and follow us."

"Do you have some sort of identification on you? How do I know you're who you say you are?"

"Are you expecting someone else?"

"I don't know what to expect down here. So far, I'm not real impressed with how things are run. Do you have any ID with you?"

One of the men patted a bulge under his shirt and connected to his belt. Anyone who had ever seen a Dirty Harry movie would know that that gesture indicated that he had a gun under his shirt and that he expected David to do exactly as he was told. David's mind was racing, and the conclusions he was drawing weren't very pleasant. This had to have something to do with the incident in Mexico a few days earlier. He knew it would not be wise to go anywhere with these two, but at the moment they were holding all the cards. With every step as they left the ferry and walked up the parking area, their courtesy disappeared. They obviously were not representing any government. They were thugs and probably on El Dorado's payroll.

"Where are we going?"

"No questions, gringo. You are going where we tell you. We have a good friend still suffering from a broken jaw who wants very much to speak with you."

David could feel his heartbeat speeding up by the second. He was growing increasingly nervous not knowing what to expect and envisioning the worst. They would probably take him to meet the guy that Tom had smacked with the board and, after beating him up five times worse, would finish the job by blowing his brains out and throwing his body into the ocean. He certainly wasn't expecting what was waiting.

The two thugs pushed him across the road to a small field where a very sleek, black helicopter sat. As they approached, the pilot spotted them and engaged the rotors causing a blast of wind to throw sand up into his face. Before shoving him into the back seat compartment, one of the two men took a large electrical tie and bound David's hands together behind his back. They didn't bother to throw his bag onboard. They left it sitting in the field.

One of his custodians took the front seat opposite the pilot and the other sat in the back next to him. In seconds they were airborne. He knew this wouldn't have a happy ending. It was ironic that he was probably going to be killed just as he had realized what the most important things in his life were. What a shame that he wouldn't have the chance to tell his sons how he felt about them or to try to mend fences with his wife. It was unlikely anyone would ever know what had happened to him. They would never even have a body to bury. They were more than likely just going to push him out of the aircraft once they were out to sea. He had to ask himself though, why a petty crook would have the use of such an expensive piece of equipment. It didn't make sense. He would have his answer quickly enough.

After several high-banked turns, the chopper began its descent. Ahead, David could see a very large motor yacht, perhaps over two hundred feet long, with a chopper landing deck on its stern. The helicopter moved slowly and deliberately to the landing pad. Waiting beside the pad on the deck was a familiar face, albeit with the addition of a major bandage wrapped around his neck and jaw. Before David could exit the chopper, someone grabbed one of his legs and pulled him out so he fell onto the steel deck. He proceeded to kick David repeatedly and as hard as possible. David tried to curl up and protect his face. That left the sides of his head and his back wide open for punishment. The guy hammered him repeatedly until one of his accomplices pulled him away, and said in Spanish, "Don't kill him yet. He's got to be able to answer some questions before you end his days. Get him up and let's take him below."

David was in great pain. His kidneys and one ear had taken the brunt of the beating and he could feel warm liquid running down the side of his face. He couldn't reach up to wipe it away with his hands still bound. One of the morons with him took a towel and crudely swiped it across his head. In the second it spent on his head, it came back completely soaked in blood. He knew he had suffered some bad cuts, but was so numb from the beating that he wasn't even feeling the damage yet. He knew it would be coming soon. They pushed him in front of them to what had to be the galley in a lower cabin area. They pulled a straight-backed chair over and shoved him into it.

"Don't move or I'll let my friend here resume his tearing you in two. Sit still and don't talk."

David sat in the chair for what seemed like an hour. The pain grew steadily as he sat. He heard voices and footsteps approaching from the hallway. The door swung open and three men entered the room. The two who entered first had the unmistakable look of Mexican gang members that someone had overdressed in a failed attempt to make them blend in with a group of businessmen. The last man to enter was definitely a cut above the first two. He was polished and had an air of *noblesse oblige* about him. He thought he was special. He smiled his overly-toothy smile and walked proudly to where David was seated.

"My friend, you are a bloody mess. Sanchez, release his hands if you will and hand him a wet towel. Why, I don't even know your name. What is your name, Señor?"

"David."

"David who?"

"David Pfefferkorn."

"Well, David, you certainly are in a spot here, aren't you? I think you'll find I'm a very direct person, and we should have no trouble talking to one another. I ask you a question, you answer truthfully, and we keep going 'til I run out of questions or you run out of truth. You answer everything I'm asking you one hundred percent truthfully and you might walk away from all this. Of course, that will be after our friend with the busted jaw finishes his retributions. You lie to me, even once, and, well, you'll wish you were dealing with him instead of me."

"Sanchez, give him the damp towel so he can wipe some of that disgusting blood off his face and hands. How many times do I have to ask you?"

David's head and back were now hurting as if he had been in a car wreck. This was the last thing he needed, to be grilled by a madman while he was in excruciating pain.

"There, that's much better. Can we get you something to drink, a smoke? Anything, my friend, you just ask and I'll have it brought to you."

"I could use some water."

"Done. Sanchez, please, a cold water for David."

David drained the water in two swallows, even though his throat hurt from the kicking. His inquisitor smiled and started again. "Now, David, let me tell you a little about me. My name is Ernesto Lopez. No one calls me that. My very close friends do call me Ernesto, but most everyone else calls me by my professional name El Dorado. Perhaps you have heard of me?"

"Yes, I know who you are. What do you want with me? I've never run drugs or broken any laws, other than a speed limit, in my life. I'm not involved in your business."

"Oh, but you are. You are very involved. I'll show you. First, let's see how truthful you are. Sanchez here will run my lie detector and you and I will talk. Now, David, let's start with a few baseline questions. Where are you from?"

"New Bern, North Carolina, on the coast."

"That's not what my records show. They indicate you are from Winston-Salem. You remember what I said about lying to me don't you? Don't try me."

"I'm not. I was born and raised in Winston, but I've been living in New Bern for the past fifteen years. It's the truth."

"Is that correct, Sanchez?"

"Yes, Señor. He has a home in New Bern. He could live there."

"Okay, David. Do you have a family?"

"Two sons and a wife. We're separated right now. I was going back home to try and patch things up with her."

"How sweet. What kind of cars do you have?"

"Why do you need to know that?"

"I might be interested in a trade. Just answer the question."

"I have an old Toyota pickup truck and my wife's SUV is still in my name."

"Sanchez?"

"Sí, he is being truthful."

"How can you tell if I'm telling the truth without even having me hooked up to anything? How does that work?"

"It's the best lie detector ever. You see, in my many businesses, most of which are perfectly legitimate, I have to run background checks on clients. So I'm a member of the credit bureau. I have access to everyone's credit file. I know more about you than you do. The computer never forgets, and the credit bureau and I never forgive. Hard to believe, eh? Now, just a few more questions. How long have you worked for Bones?"

"I don't work for him at all. I never have. I sell boats for a living back in North Carolina. I'm just down here with some buddies on a sailing trip. He offered to let us take his boat out if he could come with us. We got hit by the hurricane and just wound up in Mexico. I think he's nuts. He just wanted a crew to help him look for treasure. I'm trying to leave and go home to my family."

"Treasure? My word. If what you say is true, then you have been most unlucky. Here you sit all bloody and with someone waiting to beat you to death right behind you. And all you wanted to do was to go sailing with your friends?"

"That's right. I wish we'd never run into Captain Bones. Nothing has gone right since we met him. All this ridiculous talk about treasure got us sucked into this."

"Bones is a little nuts, but he's not crazy, and there most certainly is a treasure."

"There is Mayan gold around here?"

"There could be, but that's not the treasure Bones is looking for. He's looking for millions of dollars in cash that my old partner Nathan Hibbs stole."

"Hibbs was your old partner? In what business?"

"He was the stateside half of my most profitable import-export business."

"You mean drugs, right?"

"I've never been in the drug business. But to answer your question, anything I was in that did business in the States, Hibbs was my partner. He was my partner for about twenty years 'til he decided he didn't need any more money, or me. He took his girlfriend and my money and split."

"How was Bones tied up with this?"

"Bones worked for Hibbs. He was responsible for all of his special assignments."

"What sort of special assignments?"

"In any business, you naturally acquire enemies. These are primarily very greedy people, much like your senators back in the

States. They'll do anything for money. For that reason, they are very dangerous. They'll take you out, unless you get them first. That's where our friend Bones comes into the picture."

"Bones was a hit man?"

"Where do you think he got the nickname Bones? You didn't really think he was a pirate now did you?"

"I can't believe that. He's so small. He's got an artificial leg and everything."

"Legs don't pull triggers. And it doesn't take a very big finger either. He was the best in the business for my money. But don't look at Nathan or me for creating Bones. He was doing that for a living when Nathan met him. He was working for the government, your government. Nathan just offered him a lot more money and he jumped ship, if you'll pardon the pun."

"If all of what you say is true, then what did he need us for? Especially, if there isn't any gold."

"He hides in plain sight and even you never suspected that the old, one-legged, bearded dwarf they met in a bar is a trained killer. However, he is on a lot of lists, and that means he has no driver's license and no passport. In short, he needs to get around on that old boat, and he needed you and your friends to help him take that old piece of crap back to where he hid Nathan's money."

"How did he get hold of the money?"

"Ah, good question. We should ask that one of Nathan Hibbs. Unfortunately, Nathan fell overboard. Oh yes, and it seems that his lady friend also fell overboard at that same time. Most interesting coincidence, I'd say. The only eyewitness to the unfortunate accident was our Captain Bones. He always swore they were washed overboard together and that he had absolutely no idea that Nathan had acquired almost all of our money. That was about fifteen years ago. Of course, their bodies were never found; disposal was a specialty of Bones'. We've been keeping an eye on Captain Bones all these years waiting for him to go fetch our money. I'd say that now that you have been so kind as to help him, your friends are at risk of being washed overboard, as well, if you understand my meaning."

"Good Lord. That's the most unbelievable story I think I've ever heard."

"David, look around you. The boat you're sitting in cost over thirty million dollars. I had it custom made in the States. I'm not the kind of person who takes the time to make up stupid stories. Now, I have one last question for you. As you can see, I've not held back anything from you, and I hope you'll be as courteous with me. Exactly where is Bones and the boat? I'm certain you know."

"If I tell you what I know and you find the boat, what will you do with my friends?"

"If they are still alive when I get my money back and you live up to your word, then you and your friends can take the old boat and sail home. You have my word on it. I don't need anything from you. What do you say?"

"I think we can work this out. If I tell you where they are, then you let me off the boat and I am free to go?"

"To be honest with you, I will most definitely let you off the boat. I won't come after you at all. However, a lot of the men who work with me are what you might call independent contractors. The man whose face you crushed is in that category, and I do not control his every action. I know that is contrary to what many folks might say about me, but that is the truth. So, you leave the boat and find a way to get away from him, then what you do is your business."

"You have a deal. Bones and the *Dark Lady* are anchored on the back side of Ambergris Caye."

"There's no harbor there. I've been all over Ambergris."

"Yes, there is. It's very tiny and there's only a small break in the reef to get into it. Bones knew it well. He said the treasure was located near that area. You'll find him there; I promise you."

"I believe you, David. It was a pleasure doing business with you. Can I get you anything before I go?"

"Nope. I just want to get my shot at getting out of here."

"I understand. Sanchez, please see that our friend David gets off the boat safely. You understand, Sanchez?"

"I do, Señor."

David thought he heard a double entendre between El Dorado and Sanchez, and he didn't like the sound of it. Sanchez walked David to the gangplank leading to the dock and gave a loud whistle. Waiting on the dock was the angry looking thug Tom had smashed in the face with a plank. Sanchez grabbed David by the shoulder and gave him a slight push down the gangplank.

"Good luck, Señor. I think you will need it."

David sized up the situation. It was going to be a one-on-one contest. The problem was only one of them had a pistol, and it wasn't David. He had only a second or two to come up with a plan, so he came up with the one that seemed the easiest to implement. As he touched the dock, he grabbed his chest and fell to his knees.

"Don't even try it, Señor. I will not fall for such a stupid ploy. You will come with me now, and we will settle up between us."

In response, David groaned and clasped his hands over his chest. After a few seconds, the impatient gunman came over beside him and pointed the pistol directly at his head. "You will come with me now, Señor. Stop this charade."

"I think I'm having a heart attack. I have serious heart problems. I need my pills or I'll die right here. It's the stress. I can't get up. Please, I will come with you, but let me take my nitro pill. It's in my pocket." David fumbled with his shirt pocket. His hand was shaking so badly, he couldn't grab the supposed pill.

"Here, Gringo. I'll grab the pill. You'll swallow it and we must go."

"I will. I always do what I say. I'll go."

The Mexican reached into his shirt pocket while holding the gun firmly with his other hand. No sooner had he reached into David's shirt pocket than David made his desperate move. He reached up quickly, grabbed the barrel of the pistol in his massive paw, and fell back over the dock wall holding the gun and the gunman tightly.

"You are crazy. I will blow your brains out for this."

"I suggest you let the gun fall, or you can drown for all I care. I have a huge advantage over you right now."

"What are you talking about, gringo?"

"Captain of the Navy Swim Team, Hawaii, 1969. You're in my back yard now."

Immediately upon hitting the water, David started kicking, diving down deep under the surface, and still holding onto the thug. It was only a matter of seconds before the gasping gunman dropped his weapon and tried to break away. David thought to himself that this creep was lucky he was not a killer. He could have held onto him just long enough to make certain he had a nice swallow or two of water in his lungs prior to surfacing. Instead, David grabbed him by his hair, then, using the firemen's crawl, paddled him to land. He pulled him up on the muddy bank and spoke to him in no uncertain terms. He realized if David hadn't held onto him, he wouldn't have been able to make it to shore.

"If I were the animal you are, I would have killed you. I'll let you live this time, but you owe me. Don't cross me again, or I will finish you off."

David walked briskly away from the still gasping and nearly drowned man. As he looked back over to the mega yacht, he saw that crewmembers were tossing off lines and easing her out of port. No one needed to tell him where the yacht was headed. He needed to get back to the *Dark Lady* and his friends as quickly as he could find a way.

10

Bones insisted that Triste be left on *Dark Lady* as a watch. To my mind, I didn't know which of the two options was the more dangerous. If El Dorado or his crew found our ship, it would not be good for Triste to be aboard. However, it was not difficult to see that the shore looked like a dense jungle and it probably had a lot of things living there that would find our presence disturbing.

If anyone approached, he was to ring the ship's bell as loudly as he could. If that didn't get a response from our landside treasure hunting crew, then he was to shoot a round off from the ship's flare gun. He was proud to be trusted with the ship, even though the rest of us were a little nervous about leaving him behind. He was a serious and competent young man, but that didn't stop us all from being apprehensive about him remaining alone. Tom made two quick trips with the dinghy to get the group ashore before heading down the coast with David. Once on the beach we began walking in a loosely knit group down a narrow path that could only be described as a game trail.

After returning from dropping David off, Tom pulled the dinghy up on shore and into some bushes. We hadn't gone a half a mile before he caught up with us. He told us, as we trekked toward a very dense swamp, that David was really excited about heading home when he had left him on the beach. There was dark water on both sides of our path, and I didn't need anyone to remind me that there were crocodiles in this part of the world. For my taste, the edge of the water was a little too close to the edge of the trail. I was getting a headache from looking at every bush and tree, just waiting for the croc or snake or God knows what to jump out at us. As thick and overgrown as the underbrush was, it was what I had always envisioned a tropical rainforest to be. The amount of noise coming from the birds, monkeys, and other animals was remarkable.

I noticed that Bones was headed in a very specific direction. He didn't have the supposed treasure map anywhere in sight, so I could only assume he had it memorized. He led the group with a machete in his hand, swinging it at the overgrown vines and bushes, making the path a little easier to traverse.

I could tell the denseness of the jungle was making the ladies nervous. Susanne was practically in my shoes with me, and Karen was similarly on Tom's back. The fact was, I enjoyed being her rock; she could lean on me all she wanted. When this adventure was over and we returned to Florida, I was going to ask her to move in with me. I wasn't all that much to look at with my bald head and middle-aged paunch but I had the heart of a lion, or at least a bobcat, and I was really drawn to her.

Bones yelled back to the group, "Okay, folks, we've got a croc over here on the starboard side. He's a big one and not all that far away from the path. I'll stand right here and you pass behind me."

As we moved behind Bones, we could clearly see a crocodile well over ten feet long, staring at us. He looked almost like a statue, as he didn't so much as blink while we all passed by him. I felt like he was reading a menu at a fine steakhouse and contemplating how delicious the meal was going to be. Though his mouth was closed, it was easy to spot the two-inch long, razor-sharp, teeth running along the seam of his mouth. I was thankful Bones had spotted him.

As we plodded along through the jungle, one more obstacle was added to the journey. Rain. It started as a light drizzle and within ten minutes had escalated to a tropical downpour. The steam rising up from the jungle floor made staying on the path difficult, simply because we had difficulty even seeing it. The last thing we needed to do was get a little bit closer to the water's edge. I could feel it every time we passed a small branch of water – we were being watched by hungry eyes.

Bones tried to instill a little confidence in his troops, "Not to worry. According to the map we'll be at a landmark in a short while."

"What map are you following, Bones? I haven't seen you look at one yet."

"Got it committed to memory. You got to remember; I've been staring at that map for years. I know it like the back of my hand, maybe better. Trust me, I'll get you there."

"We're right behind you, and I don't think we could turn around and find our way back even if we wanted to."

Susanne pulled up close behind me. I knew that despite her being a strong woman, she was a little unnerved marching in the rain through a jungle. I noticed Tom had gathered up Karen to lend the same bit of security to her. Tuna, well, he brought up the rear and seemed to be enjoying the walk. He was the kind of guy that never showed a lot of emotion either way, excited or nervous. He was the quintessential scientist to the end. I just hoped our end wasn't any time soon.

As we continued our trek, a thought crossed my mind. "Bones, how come we didn't bring any equipment with us? Won't we need a shovel to dig for the gold? Surely, it's not just sitting up on top of the ground."

"Not a problem." He patted the small duffel bag he had swung over his shoulder.

"Got most anything we'll need in this little bag right here. The treasure is hidden all right, but we don't need shovels to find it. According to the map, it's in a water-filled cave. At high tide, it's actually not accessible. We've got to get moving. When the tide starts coming in and backing up the water into the cave, we'll be in serious trouble. Whatever we're doing in the cave, we need to be finished shortly after that, or we'll be buried for eternity along with the treasure."

"I wish I hadn't asked. This gets worse by the minute."

"Like I said, I've got it all figured out. Trust me and we'll all be fine, and rich."

* * *

David clearly understood the severity of the situation. He was drenched and he had no dry clothes, money, papers, or help. He was in a strange city and realized that El Dorado and company had all of those things and, undoubtedly, assistance from the local government. He racked his brain trying to come up with a common sense solution to a very uncommon situation. As if he was smacked in the face with a wet towel, it hit him. He was already in the best place possible to look for help. He was a sailor in dire need of help, and there's no more ready group to lend help to a sailor, than other sailors. He looked around the harbor for the largest grouping of masts and headed for the small marina with a decent collection of sailboats.

As he approached the first group of boaters, he noticed they were sitting under a veranda at the marina having their first beer of the day. He walked toward them and immediately one of the ladies in the group of about five stood up and asked him, "Sweetheart, what on earth happened to you? Did you fall off your boat? Here, let me get you a towel." The woman grabbed a beach towel from her bag and went over to David and pulled up a lawn chair for him. "You sit right here and let me look at that ear. Goodness, you could use a couple of stitches. What did you hit?"

"This is a long story, and I don't have time to tell it all to you. Here's the situation in a nutshell. It's going to seem unbelievable, and that's fine, since I'm finding it sort of hard to believe myself. Here goes. I'm with a crew of three other guys, two women, our insane captain, and one kid. We're on a large schooner which is anchored off of Ambergris Caye in a remote lagoon. My friends, the ladies, and the kid are all in a lot of danger, as it turns out our captain is part of a drug cartel from Mexico, and he ran off with a ton of their money. I was leaving, going back home to North Carolina, when the guys he stole the money from grabbed me, beat the crap out of me, and left me with a thug who tried to kill me. That didn't go well for him, so here I am. I don't have any money or identification, and I need to get back to Ambergris to warn my friends. They have no clue what is really happening. They think they're looking for Mayan gold."

The oldest sailor in the group stood up and walked over to David. He willingly extended his hand to shake David's. "My name is Ed, Ed Browning. My friends call me Brownie. I'm from Annapolis and I'm here, like the rest of these folks, on my boat. I've heard a lot of sailor tales in my time, but this one is really out there. You say you're a sailor from North Carolina, is that right?"

"That's right."

"Okay, before I'm willing to get involved in all this mess, I want to ask you a few questions. You alright with that?"

"You a member of the Credit Bureau, too?"

"What do you mean?"

"Bad joke. I'll explain later. Sure. Ask away."

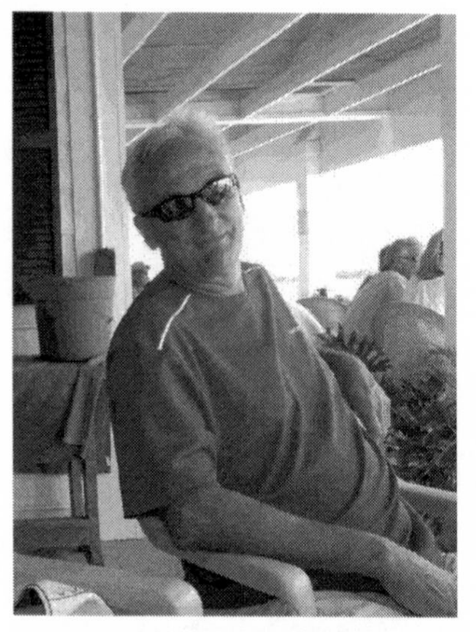

Ed "Brownie" Browning

"What town in North Carolina are you from?"

"New Bern, on the Neuse River."

"What is the small village downriver from New Bern where everybody loves to spend the night on their way down the ditch to Florida?"

"You mean Oriental?"

"That's right. Okay, just a couple more. See that large boat over there on the T dock? What kind of rig does it have?"

"It's a ketch, a Morgan Forty-One Out Island."

"You're a sailor alright. One last question. Who won the last America's Cup?"

"The Oracle team, Larry Ellison."

"I'm sold. Anybody else have a question?"

No one volunteered, so Brownie continued, "What do you think we need to do?"

"I don't think the police will help. They've been on board with the drug guys every step of the way. We need to get back to *Dark*

Lady, the schooner, as quickly as possible. If we can just save my friends, I don't care about anything else. There was a huge yacht down the dock a little while ago."

"They pulled out about twenty minutes back."

"That's the one they had me on. The guy that runs the drug cartel owns it. They are headed out to the Caye, and I'm afraid everyone there is in trouble."

"We can't possibly outrun that boat in our sailboats. It's thirty miles or so. They'll make it there in about two or three hours. It would take us three times that long. But I do have a friend down the beach that does tours on his seaplane. It seats six and I'm sure I could lean on him a little to help. Hell I've been buying him beers for the last month, he'll have to lend a hand. Let's go check him out."

Brownie, David, and Ted Clark, another sailor from the group, commandeered the dock master's golf cart and started down the narrow beach road to a small dock at the end of the harbor. Tied up to the far end of the dock was a very old seaplane. In worn letters on the side was painted *Guilfoyle Aviation, Sightseeing and Island Hops*. David was a little surprised at its age and condition.

"You sure this thing will fly? It looks like something the Red Baron might have flown."

"It's old, but he takes people up in it every day, and he ferries a lot of folks out to the Caye. He's a good guy. You'll like him."

The three men found the owner of the plane just across the street from the dock, sleeping in a hammock suspended between two palm trees. To David, he looked like Humphrey Bogart in the "African Queen." Brownie led the guys over to the sleeping pilot.

"Hey, Guilfoyle, wake the hell up. We got a mission for you."

"What are you talking about, Brownie? I'm in the middle of my nap. Don't have a charter this afternoon and after all those beers you plied me with last night, I need to sleep it off."

"Pay-back time. We've got a sailor in distress here. You've got to fly us out to Ambergris Caye immediately. He has some friends out there in trouble."

"What kind of trouble?"

"The usual. Crooked cops, drug cartels, hijacked crew."

"I wish I hadn't asked."

"What do we need to do to get underway? Time is critical."

"First, I need to fuel up, and I'm afraid my credit card is maxed out at the moment. Then I need to pump out the port float so we don't fly in circles. It leaks a little. That's about it."

"Let's get moving. We can use my card to fuel up."

The rescue team helped to untie the plane. Kevin Guilfoyle tried to fire up the engine, but encountered another problem. "Damn battery. I'll need to charge it or get a jump."

"You got jumper cables?"

"Sure do. I've been having this problem a little while. Batteries are so damned expensive."

"Here, I'll hook it up to the golf cart. It's got two six-volt batteries. I can run them together for twelve volts. Is that what you need?"

"That's affirmative."

In short order, the battery was jumped, Kevin got the plane started and taxied over to the fuel dock to top it off. By then, the yacht had a good hour and half lead on the group. They had no time to waste.

Kevin Guilfoyle – our rescue pilot

David didn't find it reassuring when the plane backfired and spit out black smoke as they headed out over the Caribbean Sea. He was concerned that they wouldn't get to the *Dark Lady* before El Dorado. Kevin chewed tobacco as he piloted, and in a few minutes, it was clear what all those brown streaks down the pilot's side of the fuselage were. Kevin pointed about ten degrees to the right.

"Is that the one you're talking about? The yacht headed to Ambergris?"

"That's it. Will we beat them out there?"

"Wow. Looks like a cruise ship. No problem. They'll be at least thirty minutes behind us. It looks like there's a front moving in from the Caye. They're getting some heavy rain and lightning. It ain't going to be fun to fly into that. We need to get down before it gets any worse. Feel the wind starting to hit us? Where do you need to go? I'll have to find a place to set us down."

David scanned the Caye until he saw two masts sticking out above the tree line on the far end of the island. "There she is. Off to the right at the very tip of the island."

Kevin banked the plane quickly. "Got it. Okay, we're going to do a quick look-see over the place and try to find a place to land the old girl."

Kevin came in just over the mast tops of *Dark Lady*. On the deck they could clearly see Triste. He was looking up at them and was alarmed at how low they were flying. Triste ran to the companionway and started ringing the alarm bell. After a minute and no response he got the flare gun out and shot it off over the jungle according to the plan. The plane came in even lower over Triste. He knew what he had to do.

Kevin made a long slow turn out to sea and then took a dead bead on the lagoon in a glide path that would take him just alongside of *Dark Lady*. "This here lagoon is just barely long enough to land. I'm going to touch right at the shoreline and hope we can stop before we reach the other shore. Pontoons don't like sandy beaches. Okay, boys, here we go. Hold on to your asses."

The wind was rocking the small plane from side to side at a severe angle. Putting the plane down in these conditions wouldn't be easy. David gripped the sides of his seat, leaving imprints in the vinyl upholstery. The plane may have been old and the pilot a little rough around the edges, but he could fly. The rain was pounding hard against the windshield and blasts of a crosswind rocked the small plane every five seconds. It was a butt-puckering approach.

After touching down approximately ten feet off the beach, the plane shot past *Dark Lady* with only two feet separating the plane's wingtip from the boat's hull. The forward motion of the plane stopped just as the pontoons touched the sandy beach. The passengers all felt as if they had aged five years in the last fifteen seconds. Kevin pulled off his headgear and turned to check them out. "Now that wasn't so bad, was it?"

David could only think of one thing to say, "Unbelievable..."

"Thanks. My mom loves me too. Okay, let's pull an anchor out of the locker and get snugged up against the beach."

David had another priority before securing the plane. "Kevin, can you taxi us over to the boat so I can get the kid off? I don't want him there if that yacht shows up before we get back here."

"No problem."

Kevin gave the engine a little power, turned it on a dime, and headed slowly out to the schooner. "I can only get so close. I'll kill the motor and nose it right up to the stern of the boat. The pontoons are almost as long as the plane. Get him to throw us a line and then he can just shinny down the rope to you. You know what I'm talking about?"

"I think I do."

Kevin did as he had said. David stepped out of the plane's door and down onto the pontoon. He braced himself on the side of the plane and eased forward on the very narrow float. Rain was pouring down his face, and lightning was striking in just about every direction. David called for Triste numerous times with no response. Concerned, he went as far to the front of the float as he could but with his oversized frame, he couldn't make the leap to the boat. Seeing David's difficulties, one of the other sailors offered to go get Triste.

"David, come on back. I can get up there. I'm a lot smaller than you are, and it won't be a problem. Agreeing, David climbed back into the cabin and Ted took his place on the pontoon. Ted quickly maneuvered himself and launched up onto the deck of the boat. He called out repeatedly for Triste, but received no response. The remaining crew waited in the plane for about ten minutes until Ted reappeared and jumped back down to the plane. Now soaked, he climbed inside and told them, "No one's aboard. I looked everywhere. Even looked forward into the anchor locker and the engine room. He's not aboard."

David was surprised. "I know I saw him on deck when we flew low overhead. We must have scared him. I don't know how he got away. There's only one dinghy and the other guys took it to shore. He must have swum for it."

David and Ted

Kevin shook his head. "I wouldn't have done that."

"What's the problem?"

"You fly low over this lagoon when the sun's out and see the number of large sharks hanging around here all the damn time, and you wouldn't either. Not a smart move."

"I'm sure he was scared. He's a great kid, and he's probably gone to warn the others that there are people coming. He doesn't have a clue who we are."

Kevin pointed toward the beach. "That him?"

Walking ashore was a dripping wet Triste. David yelled out to him, but the wind and rain made it impossible for him to hear or see David. Triste broke out in a dead run for the trees before he could see David.

"Okay, Kevin. Better taxi back over to shore, and we'll head in after him. I don't have any idea which way they went."

"Will do. Tell you what. We can start out on one side of the lagoon and walk the shore 'til we spot their dink. Maybe we'll see some footprints if we can find where they went ashore."

"Good idea."

Kevin revved up the engine and as soon as the wind put some distance between the plane and boat, he headed back to the far end of the lagoon. This time they pulled an anchor ashore and secured the plane to the beach. Kevin looked across the lagoon at the deteriorating weather conditions.

"This is more than a squall. Looks like it's set in for a while. The jungle gets really nasty when the water gets high. We'll need to stay together and for God's sake watch where you're walking. I hate this friggin' lightning."

The would-be rescuers started walking down the beach.

11

Bones continued to take the lead, guiding the rest of us through the jungle toward a supposed treasure that we were beginning to believe didn't exist. Even though we had never been far away from the sound of waves crashing onto shore, the roar became noticeably louder and soon we found ourselves atop a bluff overlooking the sea with a good sized cliff at our feet. Near the bottom of the cliff, we could see where waves had been eating at the limestone wall for years causing massive erosion. Bones looked over the edge and then turned to us.

"We're here. You are literally standing over the treasure."

I was the first to respond, "We're standing over it? It's buried here?"

"Not buried. It's in a cave that empties into the ocean on the face of this cliff. It's been here for thousands of years, carved out of pure limestone."

"How is it that we're supposed to get into it? I mean, it's practically got a tidal wave right in front of it."

"If it was easy, it would already have been found and we wouldn't be here. The opening is actually a little above sea level. We can lower one of us down by rope and then we can get access. Or, I suggest we split up, walk the area within two hundred feet of this spot and check every inch carefully. I'm positive there's another opening on the inland side somewhere around here, but the jungle has covered it up, making it difficult to find. It would be a hell of a lot easier than hanging over the cliff. I can't do it with my bum leg, and I don't see any of you jumping forward volunteering to give it a try."

"You're right about that, Bones. We'll search topsides up here. But in this rain I just don't think we're going to find it."

"Don't even go there. We've come a long way, and we ain't going home without the gold."

There was a new edge to his voice in that declaration, and we all felt it.

Susanne whispered to me, "You don't think he's losing it, do you? You have to admit on the surface, looking at this from a hundred feet away, most folks would say we've all gone crazy to be out here. We're on a remote island, with all kinds of wild animals, in the middle of a monsoon, following a one-legged hermit looking for lost Mayan gold. Maybe it's just me."

"No, I've thought the same thing. I'm only going to do this a little bit more, and then I'm calling it a day. I never really felt this was real, but Bones always seemed like a harmless old guy with this one dream. I was willing to go along if only to be on the boat, but this is getting weirder by the minute."

As Bones requested, we broke off into teams and started to examine the ground closely. Susanne and I went one direction, Tom and Karen in another, and Bones and Tuna took a third direction. It was raining so hard that I was having trouble seeing what was ten feet in front of me. To find this needle in a haystack was a ridiculous goal. We were all leery of where to put our feet as we imagined what might be coiled around the next vine we passed. I was cold, drenched, and tired, and I could tell that the ladies had already had enough of this and they wanted nothing more than to hear that it was time to turn back for the boat. I was ready to tell

Bones it was over, but I didn't have time to voice my concerns before I heard Bones and Tuna calling for us. We followed their voices and found them in the midst of a lush, fern-covered area under a thick umbrella of tall palms. Tom and Karen came up quickly behind us.

"What's up? Ready to go back to the boat and dry off? I'd love a warm shot of brandy."

Bones smiled through his tobacco stained teeth. "It's here. Right here. Don't step beyond us. You'll fall into the sinkhole. It drops right down into the cave. It ain't big, but I think all of us can squeeze through it. We'll use my flashlight and lower ourselves down with the rope."

"Bones, what makes you so sure this is it? I mean, this looks pretty dangerous to me. I sure wouldn't want the ladies having to do this."

"It's right where the map said it would be. Didn't I say a cave? Didn't I say there was a back entrance? Am I that good a fortuneteller? It's here just like it's supposed to be. The gold is right under us, somewhere in this cave."

"Somewhere? You don't know any more than that?"

"People died here. There's no photographs or GPS charts to go by. For a treasure that's four hundred years old, I think we've done pretty damned good finding it to this point. Even Mel Fisher looked for years before he found the *Atocha*. Our treasure is on land, not on the bottom of the ocean. We just drop through here and do a little exploring. It can't be that far. The ocean is just a hundred yards away. The cave runs right to it."

Susanne made her position clear, "I'm not going down there and that's final, and I'm certain Karen won't either. We'll just go back to the boat."

"How will you find your way back?"

Tuna volunteered, "I'll go back with them. There's no need for all of us to go down there. You and Jim and Tom can check it out. I'll get them back. We'll just walk along the shoreline 'til we get back to the lagoon. It's an island. I know it's back and to the right."

"Thanks, Tuna. If we find anything, you'll all get your share."

"Okay. We're leaving. Please be careful down there."

Susanne came up and kissed me square on the lips. "Please be careful. I don't want anything happening to you."

"After that, you can be sure I'll be careful. We'll be back to *Dark Lady* soon. You stay on board 'til we get there."

As if that wasn't enough romance for an afternoon, Karen laid a big one on Tom and told him she'd be waiting with a hot shower and a warm towel. It's always great to have something to look forward to.

The three of them headed off to the beach leaving me, Tom and Bones to explore the cave. I was still very apprehensive about going down into a dark cave, especially since we could clearly hear water rushing into it from our perch above. Tom volunteered to go in first. He took the rope that Bones had brought and tied one end to a palm tree that was close to the hole in the ground. He tied the other end around his waist.

"Tom, you know Bones and I together couldn't pull you up."

"If that tree doesn't uproot, I can get myself back up. You don't know if crocodiles live under here, do you, Bones?"

"You're safe. That's salt water from the ocean. Crocs don't live in it 'cept in the Florida Keys. Here's a bright flashlight. I have a backup here in my bag if that one dies on us. Good luck."

Tom pulled a couple times on the line to make certain the knot around the tree was secure. He lowered himself into the dark hole. He had a lot more guts than I did. I would follow, but being first is tough to do. The rope stayed taut for about five minutes and then fell slack. I put my head down over the hole and yelled for Tom. He called back to me.

"I'm on solid ground. It's darker than hell, and you won't believe how fast the water's running through here. Come on down. I'll catch you at the bottom. There's a ledge down here beside the water."

Bones came over to me, "Okay, Hawkins. This is it. As soon as you get down there, tell Tom to wait on me, 'cause I know the location of the gold according to the map. It won't be easy to find. There's lots of tunnels and dead ends down there."

"You sure you haven't been down there before? It almost sounds like you have."

"Just been dreaming about it and studying the map, Hawkins. That's all. Now, you get on down there and call me when you're at the bottom. I'll be right behind you."

Descending into the darkness suspended by a small rope around my waist was as nerve racking as riding out the hurricane. Tom wasn't kidding. The water was running so strong through the cave that it caused a breeze. It wasn't raining in the cave but with all the spray, it might as well have been. The roar of the water forced us to yell to hear each other. Tom shined the light around inside and then up to the hole where Bones was doing his best to join us. His prosthetic leg caused him to struggle more than most people. He groaned and strained, but finally made it down to where we were waiting.

"Damn. That sure ain't easy. Boys, let's look around here a minute and get our bearings."

Bones took one of the flashlights he had brought and studied the interior of the long, narrow hole in the earth. As he hit portions of the dark wall with the light beam, we could clearly see moving creatures. They weren't taking step-like movements. It was definitely a slither.

"Snakes. Quite a few. Better watch where you step and where you put your hands. I don't know what kind they are, but I'd just as soon not find out if they're poisonous. Let's start walking down toward the ocean side of this thing."

As we walked single file down the narrow ledge, it became smaller with every step. It was covered with a slimy green moss that made the footing treacherous. There was no way to tell the depth of the water running through the bottom of the cave, and shining the flashlight into it didn't show a bottom. It was best to assume it was too deep to wade through.

"Is it my imagination or is the water getting higher?"

Bones replied, "It's not your imagination. As the tide rises, the water in here rises with it. We need to move faster to get to the main cave while we still have a place to walk. I don't want to have to swim for it."

"Bones, I swear you've been in here before. How do you know there's a bigger room ahead?"

"I've told you. It's all on the map. There's actually a small drawing that shows all of this. You worry way too much, Hawkins. Just keep moving and we'll be there shortly."

As we walked the water got deeper, wider and faster. The ledge got so narrow, our feet barely fit on it and, to say the least, Bones was not sure footed. We put him between us and I kept a hand on his shoulder to help him balance. In spite of our best efforts, he still took a tumble and fell head first into the raging water. Afraid we would lose him, Tom and I both dove in after him. We each grabbed an arm and held him up while the current pushed us with an amazing force toward the sea. Hoping to find a spot to get out, we moved to the side of the stream so we could grab anything that appeared able to hold us. Tom held his light above the water and shone it on the cave walls. The stream got wider and began to calm down some in response to a reverse Venturi effect. Ahead we saw a wider room and another ledge that we could use to make good our escape from the rising waters.

* * *

El Dorado's yacht slowly approached the narrow channel and entered the lagoon. The lavish boat came to within fifty yards of *Dark Lady* and dropped its anchor. Within minutes, a crew of men, including El Dorado, were aboard a high-powered motor launch and headed to the schooner. While only two of the men held automatic weapons, there was a high probability that all of the other men were also armed. The launch tied up alongside *Dark Lady*. The two most heavily armed thugs hopped aboard the sailboat and began their methodical search for anyone aboard. They reported back to their boss that the vessel was empty.

"They must all be ashore. Sanchez, you and Javier stay here with the boat. If anyone shows up, tie them up and hold them 'til I can get back and find out what they know. We'll go ashore to see if we can find Bones and my money."

The black-hulled speedboat reared up on its stern as the driver pushed the throttle forward. They were on the beach in less than a minute. In a case of superbly bad timing, Tuna, Karen, and Susanne came out of the underbrush at almost the same moment that El Dorado and crew entered. They were immediately seized by his men.

"Ladies. Finally, we are all together again. For simple schoolteachers, you seem to have an aptitude for trouble. You are lucky to be back in my care. I'm not nearly so ruthless or dangerous as your Captain Bones."

With wet hair hanging down in front of her face and clothing drenched from the torrential rain, Susanne shot back at El Dorado, "You're lucky I don't have a gun right now. And Bones has been very good to us. He helped us to get out of that cesspool you call a country."

"Ah, Bones the humanitarian. For those of us who know him well, that is absolutely hilarious. I would say 'one of the most violent men on the planet,' if I were asked to describe him. You are making me laugh. But we are in a hurry to catch up with your wonderful captain. We are going to send you ladies back to my yacht, *Diablo*, and get you into some warm, dry clothes. You, sir, what is your name?"

"Everyone calls me Tuna."

"Tuna, like the fish?"

"Yes."

"Well, you are completely wet so that is appropriate. You will be our guide back to Bones. How many men are with him?"

"Why should I tell you anything? You're probably going to kill us anyway."

"Don't assume anything, Mr. Tuna. I would think that you should be more concerned about the ladies than yourself. This is no time for selfishness. I'll ask you again, how many are with Bones, and where are they?"

"There's two men. I can take you close to where they are, but they went into a cave without us. I'll take you to the cave, but you have to guarantee me you will not harm Karen or Susanne."

"Such beautiful names. Absolutely. I am not a man who would ever harm a woman. Many lovely women actually work for me. I love women." El Dorado pointed down the cove to the beached aircraft. "Which of you came over here on the old seaplane?"

"None of us. I don't know anything about it. It wasn't here when we arrived."

"One thing, Mr. Tuna. You tell me one lie or try to escape, and my promise not to hurt anyone will be null and void." El Dorado turned to one of his henchmen. "Take them to my boat, and Tuna will lead the rest of us back to the cave."

No one standing beside El Dorado, neither Tuna nor the ladies, had any idea that David, Kevin, and his two buddies were less than a hundred feet away, watching the entire scene from behind dense palmetto bushes. Since they were not armed and El Dorado's crew was, they had wisely remained under wraps until they could come up with a plan of action. Kevin had proven to be a lot more of the soldier of fortune than David had previously thought. "Here's what I think we should do. There's just one guy with the girls. We come up on him from behind before he can get in the boat. We'll take him out quickly, before he can sound an alarm to El Dorado and company."

David was distressed by Kevin's suggestion. "Take him out? You mean, like slit his throat or something? I don't think I can do that."

"No, you've seen Rambo too many times. You watch and I'll call for you if I need help. At least we'll know the ladies are safe. We'll take this a step at a time. Pick them off in small groups. If we can take this guy out, we'll also have a weapon. We've got to get up there before they get in the boat. Since you know the girls, David, get their attention and try to get them to lead the guy back in the bushes. We need to get them to tell him they really have to use the john."

"I'll try. I'm not sure how to signal them that."

"Come up behind them, show the girls your fly, and point to the woods. They'll understand."

"You're good at this, man."

"Two years in the Middle East. Gulf War, version one. Okay, let's move in."

David and Kevin led the others as quietly as possible. With the rain still coming down strongly, it helped mask any bushes rustling. Just as the gunman was about to force the girls into the boat, David stood up behind them in the bushes and executed the zipper maneuver. Karen saw him and understood immediately. David and crew knelt back down.

"I've got to go to the toilet before we leave. I'm going to pee in my pants and all over your boss's expensive boat. Just let me walk over to the bushes and I'll use it there."

"Make it pronto. Wait for me. You go just behind that bush over there." He pointed to a nearby palmetto.

"Fine, but you turn your head. I'm not going to put on a show for you, buddy."

"Okay, lady, okay. Just get on with it."

As soon as he turned away, Kevin and David jumped him. He had only a pistol and it was tucked into a holster on his belt. They grabbed his arms and removed the pistol in less than two seconds. Susanne saw David and ran to him.

"That was incredible. Who are these guys?"

"New friends from the States by way of Belize. They're the best. Are there any more of El Dorado's morons around here?"

"Mr. Dorado said there were two on *Dark Lady,* and his captain is out there on his cruise ship."

"Kevin, any ideas for taking back our boat?"

"It's getting pretty close to dark. With all this rain, we could probably go right out there on their launch, and they'd just assume we were part of the gang."

"That makes sense. What will we do when we get there?"

"Let the girls go aboard first. Then I'll follow with my hands loosely bound like I'm tied up. Two more of us can be in the launch pretending to be his guys. One of them can wear this clown's poncho and hat, and they'll never suspect us. When they turn their back, I'll pull this gun on them, and you girls can take their weapons. What do you think?"

David was more than a little nervous about the plan, but he stepped forward just the same. "I should already be dead. I'm having a lucky run of it. I'm in."

The two guards left to watch *Dark Lady* saw the launch approaching in the falling light. They were taking a smoke break, and being on an empty boat, neither was holding his weapon. They lowered the metal boarding steps to the launch. That played perfectly into the scheme and Susanne and Karen stepped sheepishly aboard, heads down and hands bound in front of them. Kevin followed them in a similar whipped puppy posture. One of the guards shouted down in Spanish. "Is that all of them?"

Ted's New England accent was a little off the mark, but the wind and rain helped him pass with a simple, "Sí."

The two guards came over to the edge of *Dark Lady* and looked down into the launch. The first stood upright in shock when he realized that the only one onboard who was part of El Dorado's gang had his arms tied behind his back. He turned to grab his weapon only to find Kevin holding it with the barrel pointed straight at him.

"I wouldn't move there, mi amigo. I'm a little rusty with an Uzi, so I might slip up and blow your friggin' head off."

"Careful, señor. Be very careful."

"Okay. You two. Get down on your knees, hands behind your backs."

One of the two spoke no English, so Ted had to communicate with him by relaying the orders. Soon the three men were bound and gagged, back to back, and tied to the ship's mast. They would not be going anywhere without help.

* * *

El Dorado and his remaining two gunmen continued into the jungle with Tuna leading the way. The floor of the jungle was like a lake, as the hard tropical rain had been falling full force for hours. There was less than an hour of daylight left and darkness would make this journey a lot more dangerous.

12

Bones, Tom, and I rested on the ledge and looked out at the ever-rising channel of water. It was now lapping at our feet and would undoubtedly cover the ledge in a few more minutes. We had to get moving to higher ground, wherever that was, and quickly.

"Bones, we're in trouble here. It's getting dark outside; the water's still rising; and we don't know where the hell we are."

"I know where we are. We're very close to a king's ransom. Here's what we need to do: The spot we need to reach is just around the bend. It's a wide area where it's shallow and then there's a large area of no water. That's where we'll find the gold. Let's tie one end of the rope to this rock. Hawkins, you and Tom can grab the other end of the rope and hold to it. Let the water carry you around the bend and when you're at an opening just around the corner, climb out one at a time. Then, you guys can hold onto the rope, I'll untie this end from the rock and then to my waist. You guys can reel me in when I get to where you are. Just remember, I can't swim a lick with this bum leg, but I can hold my breath long enough to get to you. It's going to be pretty dark though, so I'll need one light here to get the rope free and tie it around my waist. You guys got enough guts to go for it? To tell you the truth, if we don't, we're goners for sure."

"What choice do we have?"

"None."

"That's what I was thinking. All right, Tom, I'll grab the end of the rope, and you grab it just in front of me."

It was with a tremendous amount of fear and misgivings that I grabbed the loose end of that rope. Tom gave me a big smile and grabbed on just in front of me. "Jim, let's get this done."

The water was warm and dark. It was moving quickly, and we coul+dn't touch the bottom. That was more than a little disconcerting, especially since we had seen earlier what lived around this area. In the dark like this, my imagination was running wild. It wasn't the wildlife that I should have been concerning myself with, however. Suddenly and without any apparent cause, our once-tight rope went limp. We heard Bones yelling to us, "Boys, you've been a great crew, and I appreciate you're getting me to my treasure. Unfortunately, it's right where I'm standing and you're a stumbling block to my plans. My suggestion would be to just take a deep swallow of seawater and go on to your reward. Sorry, fellas."

Tom and I were stunned by this cold-hearted and calculated revelation. Tom grabbed my shoulder, "Let's stay together. That slimy little bastard! He was planning on this all along. We just saved his ass and he does this to us? I can't believe it. If I ever get my hands on him… Any ideas on what to do to get out of here?"

"We've got to get to another ledge or somewhere to get out of the water."

With an abrupt slam, the decision was made for us. The stream went underground against the back wall of the cave, which we had just struck with considerable force. The speed of the water was trying to pull us under. That seemed like a very bad choice not knowing how far the stream might run underground.

"Let's push along the wall. If I go under, don't let me slip away."

Tom replied, "All I can say is, 'I'll try to hang on to you. Lead the way.'"

I inched along the wall, not wanting to reach out in the darkness and not wanting to go under it either. Within five minutes, we came to the realization that we were at the end of the cave and there was no way out. If the water continued to rise we would wind up drowning in this remote place where no one would ever know to look for our remains. There was only one choice.

"Tom, if we don't make it out of here, it's been good knowing you, my friend."

"Same here, Jim. Are you thinking what I'm thinking?"

"We have no choice. The only thing left for us to do is to see what's on the other side of this wall, and I'd rather do it now while we have a little breath left than try to make it when we're choking on water."

"I'll go with you."

We each took three or four deep breaths, saturating our lungs with oxygen. Knowing this could be the end, I dove down into the stream and kicked off as hard as I could to make distance immediately. I felt Tom's hand brush against my foot as I paddled for all I was worth. I don't know how fast we were moving, but I did know my lungs were going to burst if something didn't happen soon. I thought of giving up several times and settling to the bottom, but I fought against the urge each time and kept pumping my arms and legs while trying to ignore the burning in my chest. When I felt I could no longer continue, I swam for the surface hoping for the best. My head broke through the water's surface and I gasped to get a chest full of cold, dark air.

Tom surfaced beside me and choked out, "Where the hell are we?"

"Still in the cave I'm afraid, but at least we're not dead."

"That's big in my book."

"Mine too. Let's try to find the edge of the water."

We swam 'til the water got shallow enough that we could stand. We continued walking, eventually finding ourselves completely out of the water and standing on dry surface. As I tried to see anything other than darkness, I found Tom's silhouette beside me.

"There's light coming in here from somewhere."

"You're right. Seems like it's ahead of us. I can see light specks on the water a little farther down."

We walked along the edge of the stream, and it continued to get lighter as we moved. We followed the stream through this new section of the cave, occasionally slipping into the water or scraping our hands and knees on the cave floor. After a half an hour of us barely creeping through it, the cave became dramatically brighter and our spirits soared. We each subconsciously broke into a sprint as we realized that where there was light, there was a possible escape route. As we sped forward, seemingly racing the water in the stream, we could see the clear opening ahead. Our high spirits began to waver, however, as we got closer to the opening. We both noted an increase in the sound of the rushing water, an unmistakable sound. It was the sound of a very large and very high waterfall.

We crept over to the cave's mouth, taking great care not to slip on the stream bed, and were startled to see that we were about fifty feet in the air above the far end of the lagoon where *Dark Lady* was anchored. The waterfall cascaded over large, sharp volcanic rocks protruding from the jungle. Though it was our outlet to freedom, it would not be a cakewalk to exit down such a dangerous slope. I looked at Tom. We were both bleeding from scratches on every limb.

"I don't know about you, Tom, but I have three thoughts going through my head simultaneously."

"I'm sure I'm having some of the same ones. What are yours?"

"First and foremost, I want to find Bones and beat the living crap out of him. I'm ready to be out of this friggin' jungle and lastly, but no way the least, I want to get back to Susanne and make sure she's all right. I haven't been this interested in spending time with a woman in years. I think she's the one I'm supposed to be with from here on out."

"It's funny you say that. I'm with you on all three counts, but I'm wanting to see Karen, of course. Kind of funny how this has all played out."

"It is. Do you think there's anything in the lagoon we need to be concerned about?"

"Like sharks or crocodiles?"

"Those are thoughts four and five."

"I'd rather not know at this point. At least we know they're up to no good, unlike our old buddy Bones. Any suggestions on how we can get down from here?"

"I still have the rope coiled up on my belt. We can try tying it to something up here and rappelling down."

"Is the rope long enough to reach bottom? It's not is it?"

"Nope but it will get us within about twenty-five feet, maybe a little closer. From there, well, we'll just have to let go and hope we land in the water not too far from shore."

"I hate this. I don't like sharks or crocodiles or snakes or even spiders for that matter."

"Nobody does. I suggest we get a move on."

Tom tied one end of the rope to the base of a small tree growing on the edge of the cliff and dropped the other end down the cliff's face. He volunteered to go first.

"I'm the heaviest. If it holds me you're good to go. When I hit the water, I'm giving it all I've got for shore. Wish me luck."

"I hope we're both lucky. I've always heard that snakes and crocodiles get the second person. The first one stirs them up and they bite the second one."

"Just an old wives' tale, Jim. I wouldn't worry about it at all."

"Why's that?"

"We're probably not going to survive the fall anyway."

"Thanks. I feel much better now."

"No problem. I'm gone."

I watched as Tom crawled down the narrow line, hand over hand, until he reached its bottom. He hung there for a moment, as if timing his drop, and then let go. Though it was still a long drop, it was over in less than two seconds. I watched as he went under and then broke the surface. He wasted no time in burning it to shore. Apparently he survived the fall and the swim.

It was now my turn. I hated heights almost as much as I hated my thoughts of sharks and crocodiles. I grabbed the rope and, repeating Tom's efforts, climbed down to the end. It wasn't as easy as Tom made it look. With every descent, I swung out in an arc only to swing back in, pounding into the sharp rocks. It was hard to not be concerned about the amount of blood that was running down my forearms. In my mind I was quickly becoming very enticing fish food. As I reached the literal end of my rope, I looked down at the water and clearly understood Tom's apprehension of letting go. I saw large, dark shapes moving smoothly around the edges of the water. I knew only a couple of aquatic animals that were that big and none I wanted to see at this moment.

Tom looked up at me, and cupping his hands around his mouth, yelled, "No choice, buddy! Just drop and swim like hell!"

I had always thought it impossible to walk on water but after my swim to shore, I'm not so sure anymore. I must have left a wake like a speedboat's. When I hit sand, Tom reached down to help me out. I was overcome with relief that we were alive.

"Somebody should have warned me about that last step."

"Tell me about it. When I was swimming to shore, I promised myself that if I made it, I would never buy a crocodile belt again. I'm actually stunned that we both made it. And Bones, that old bastard, he was willing to let us bite the dust without a second thought. I'll tell you one thing, he doesn't want to see me again."

"To tell you the truth, Tom, I'd be just as happy if we never saw him again. We need to get to everyone else before he does. No telling what he'll be up to now."

Bones obviously felt no remorse for sending us to a watery grave. Though we had no clues about his sordid past, we now understood that he was far more dangerous than any of us could have imagined.

* * *

As he let the rope loose that was his safety net, Bones calmly stepped back to a rock on the back of the ledge. As he pushed the rock aside, he said aloud, "They weren't bad fellas. I just don't need them anymore. Old Bones has finally succeeded in securing his future."

Behind several large rocks, covered with branches was a large strongbox. To the side was something a little more macabre: a completely bleached out skeleton laying against the cave wall as if it were watching over the chest. Bones acknowledged its presence, 'How are you Nathan, my dear old friend? Thanks so much for looking out for my money. I notice that your girlfriend is still waiting for you over in the corner. She's certainly lost some weight. I never liked her. If it hadn't been for her, you wouldn't be here like this. You needed attention from a pretty young thing and were willing to throw everything and everybody aside to get her. Nothing quite like friends, is there? If you had just been willing to cut old Bones in for a decent share of the loot, you and I would be a long way from here today. You and your bimbo would still be sailing on *Dark Lady*, and I'd be on some tropical island with a dark haired beauty waiting on me hand and foot. Too bad. I truly hated having to do this to you, but you left me no choice. Besides, you've been here having the money all to yourself this past fifteen years. Now, it's my turn.'"

Bones took a key from his pocket and shined the flashlight at a large rusted lock that secured the strongbox. After a few minutes of turning to no avail, the lock finally broke open. Bones reached inside and as his fingers made contact with the huge stack of bills, he shuddered as if in the throes of ecstasy.

"And now, it's time to leave you here, Nathan. Don't worry. I'll have a drink to you when I reach Bora Bora. You always said you wanted to sail to there."

Bones took the large stack of bills out of the box and loaded them into his gym bag. It had straps on it so he could pull it over his shoulders like a backpack to help support the weight. After the packing was done and he had the sack secured to his back, he reached over his head to the cave ceiling. There, a large wooden board hung down from an overhead crack in the cave's roof. As he rocked the board, small stones started falling to the stream below. As he continued to rock the board, the falling debris grew larger. After ten minutes of pushing the board, the ceiling let go and dropped a large collection of rocks into the stream. Simultaneously, rays of soft light illuminated the still falling rain as it fell into the cave. Bones removed the remaining blockage, and within a few minutes, he was standing outside the cave with his sack of money.

He reveled at the success of his endeavor, "If I have to say it, this worked out even better than I thought it would. Goes to show that good planning is critical."

Night was falling quickly and the rain continued, though not nearly as heavily as before. Bones knew where he was headed. He moved toward the edge of the cliff that Tom and I had just escaped, but he had the advantage of knowing a much safer way down to the water's edge. He pushed through the underbrush and about a half-mile down the edge of the overhang, he located a stone path that wound its way down toward the base. Raising the bag of money over his head, Bones began the steep descent over the wet, slippery rocks. Below he could see the beach where he would make his escape. After what could only be deemed a herculean effort by a man with only one leg who was carrying an overstuffed bag that weighed almost as much as he did, Bones finally touched down on the soft, wet sand.

The trail of human debris he left behind him played no part in the pictures currently playing out in his mind. He would soon be the richest guy in paradise. Never again would he do the dirty work for people who kept all the money for themselves. It was all starting to pay off.

As he continued on his journey, he heard a familiar voice calling to him from above, "Bones, Bones. It's me, Triste."

Bones stopped in his tracks and looked up to the top of the cliff to see the boy being manhandled by El Dorado's henchmen and El Dorado himself. The henchmen pushed Triste to the very edge of the overhang. Only a large arm around his neck kept him from flying off the cliff to a certain death.

"Bones, my old friend. I have one of your shipmates here. He's been all over the jungle looking for you. Lucky I came along or he might have become dinner for one of the more violent residents of this island. I, of course, understand that you are the most dangerous creature here. The question is, do you want me to hand the young lad over to you? He says you are his friend and that you will speak up for him. Is that so?"

"You know I don't have any friends. Doesn't mix well in my line of work. You can have the boy."

"I don't want him. I thought he might mean something to you. If you say you don't want him, then that makes two of us. What do you say I just give him a little push over the edge?"

Triste struggled hopelessly against his captors. His feet only brushed the thinnest of the rocks lying on the precipice. If the arm around him were to let go, he was dead. Bones' first instinct was to run. He was out of their reach at the bottom of the cliff. He could easily get back into the jungle where he was more familiar with the surroundings than anyone present. But there was this young boy begging for his life above him. He knew that El Dorado was capable of killing a kid; it would not have been El Dorado's worst crime. A single life meant nothing to him if it gained him something he wanted, and he wanted the bag of money on Bones' back.

Triste begged for help, "Captain Bones, please help me. I don't want to die. If they drop me, I'll die. Please do what they want."

Bones looked up at El Dorado. "Let him go. He's just a kid. He's no use to you."

"Ah, I think he is. I think you'll swap that bag of my money for him. That's what I think."

"The boy don't mean anything to me."

"Have it your way. Eduardo, drop the boy off the cliff."

Triste again begged for his life, "Please, Bones. Please help me."

For the first time in a very long time, Bones could not let someone he knew suffer. As bad as he hated to admit it, he had grown attached to the kid. In many ways, he reminded him of himself as a kid. He was young, without anyone on his side and about to die a violent death. Bones thought he might be able to negotiate his way out of this. Or at least make an effort. Then, whether the boy survived or not, he could at least say he tried.

"Okay, you win. You can have the money. Let the kid go and you can have it."

"I wish I trusted you enough to think it was that simple, Bones, but I've known you far too long. I'm going to lower this rope to you. You will tie the bag to the end of it, and when it arrives up here, we'll let the kid go."

"Fine. Send the rope down."

With darkness spreading fast and a light rain still causing a steam-like cloud over the jungle, El Dorado personally dropped the loose end of the line to Bones. Bones took the rope and tied it to a handle on the end of the bag. "Okay, it's on. Take it."

El Dorado couldn't help but smile as he pulled the bag up over the side of the cliff. As it neared the top, he gave the order to his henchman. "Let the boy go."

Tom and I watched from the jungle's edge as the creep holding Triste let go his choke hold and quickly pushed him off the cliff. It was a surreal moment as he tumbled mid-air, head over feet into the lagoon. The tide was emptying the basin at a tremendous speed, and Triste had been knocked unconscious by the impact. His limp body raced away from the shore and Bones watched as Triste passed by the shore where he was standing. He looked up at El Dorado. "You always were a worthless bastard, and stupid."

* * *

Perplexed by Bones' statement, the drug lord looked down at the bag that was sitting at his feet just as Bones yanked on his rope that was tied to the other handle of the bag. Bones pulled it so hard, that it almost pulled El Dorado over the cliff's edge. In almost the same instance, Bones pulled his nine-millimeter Glock from his belt, knelt down on one knee and coolly blasted a shot. Even in the rain and fog from over sixty feet away, we could see that he hit El Dorado's henchman, the one who had dropped Triste, squarely in the forehead. He dropped like a stone and fell over the cliff, bouncing off the outcropping of rocks several times before hitting the water.

Despite having the prosthetic leg, Bones dove into the water and swam as hard as he could toward Triste's lifeless form. It was difficult to see how he would be able to help Triste given his own obvious struggle to stay above water. Nonetheless, he caught up to the boy and rolled him over so that his face was out of the water. It was painful to watch him try to swim and carry the youngster. We truly didn't think they would make it. Bones spotted us on the bank of the lagoon and yelled out to us, "Boys, I'm not going to make it alone. You've got to swim out to help me. I can't keep going."

Tom and I watched as Bones continued to struggle to bring Triste to shore. It was hard to forget he had not only tried to kill us, but he had also just shot a man between the eyes. But Triste needed our help and this was his only chance.

The lifeless body of Bones' gunshot victim was attracting a new sort of problem to the mix. A large fin, a very *large* fin was clearly circling the body less than fifty feet from Bones and Triste. I didn't know if I had what it took to jump in to help.

Tom looked at me. "If we're going to do this, it's got to be done this moment, or we'll be too late to help."

I don't know where it came from, but I heard myself answer, "I'm with you."

We both waded out a few feet until the water dropped off over our heads, and then we swam hard toward Bones. Triste was out but he wasn't dead. Still, this meant that he would be dead weight in the water. Since Tom was a very big guy and a strong swimmer, he volunteered to take Triste. "I've got him. You see if you can pull Bones in using the bag as a float."

As I reached for the handle on the gym bag, Bones voiced his concern about the situation. It was almost unbelievable considering the dire circumstances he was in. "That's my bag. I'm not letting it go. I still have a gun, Hawkins, and I'll use it."

I was not enthusiastic about helping him and was ready to turn around now that I understood what kind of man he really was. "Bones, your choice. I'll let it go and you can carry it to your grave, or you let go of the gun and I'll take you to shore."

"I'm not dropping the gun. You'll take me in or I'll just blow your head off."

He saw my eyes open wide as I spotted the huge fin coming up directly behind him. He had a far worse problem than me. I still offered him a choice, "You better drop the damned gun and hold on, or that shark coming up behind you is going to be the one to take you swimming."

Bones turned and was confronted by the reality of a ten-foot hammerhead that was bearing down on him. "Get me in! I'll drop it. See, I let it go. Swim, for God's sake. Don't let it get me!"

I started swimming for all I was worth. I made no effort to look back. I had about thirty more feet to make shore, and I was giving it all I had. I could hear Bones straining to paddle behind me. I thought we would make it, but the shark had other designs. There was a huge pull against the bag, and I knew that it had grabbed

Bones. I looked back just in time to see the monster shark pull Bones under. He never screamed. It was surreal how easily the shark took him. The last I saw of Bones was his one hand as it disappeared under the water. I wasted no time making for shore. I made the last twenty feet in under ten seconds, I'm sure. As I waded ashore, completely spent, physically and emotionally, I saw that Tom had already made it and was pumping Triste's chest to revive him. I had just experienced the most traumatic ten minutes of my entire life. I walked over to Tom and Triste. Will he make it?"

"I believe so. He's already coughed up water a couple of times. He's getting some air into his lungs."

I sat down on the sand next to Tom while he continued working with Triste. I looked up to the top of the cliff and saw Tuna, standing beside El Dorado with a pistol in his hand.

"Tuna, you okay?"

"I'm fine. Should I plug this guy and throw him in the drink with the other moron?"

"Let's not shoot anybody else. There's a path down to the beach just a ways down the edge of the cliff. I'll meet you there. But if he does anything stupid, you can go ahead and shoot him. God knows no one deserves it more than him."

Triste began to come around. It was a relief to hear him talk to us. "Jim. Tom. Are we safe?"

"We are."

"Did you guys save me?"

It was gut check time. We knew now just what a rotten scoundrel Bones was; certainly not the harmless old dreamer we signed aboard with. He was someone who could take a life in the blink of an eye without a second thought or any remorse. It would have been easy to take credit for saving Triste and let Bones disappear with the tide of our memories. But it was the truth that he had saved the boy and Triste could certainly use a hero.

"We helped. It was Captain Bones who shot the guy who threw you over the cliff, and who kept you afloat 'til we could swim out to you. Bones saved your life. Unfortunately, he couldn't save his own. We tried to help him, but he didn't make it."

"He drowned?"

I almost answered his question with the truth but had a second thought, "Yes. With the bad leg, he just couldn't stay on top. We tried to help him, but it didn't work."

"He was a good man, wasn't he, Jim?"

Here was another question I wasn't really sure how to answer. For most of his life he wasn't a good man, but in the end he showed he had a small part of him that was worth saving.

"Yes, Triste. He was a good man."

I looked down at the soaking wet gym bag that meant so much to Bones, that he gave his life for it. "Let's see what was worth the lives of so many people."

The bag was old and the zipper was full of sand. I strained while pulling for several moments before the zipper finally broke free. I pulled the sides apart and looked inside. The first thing to catch my eye was a tool of Bones' trade, another automatic pistol. Underneath that, however, was something a lot more valuable.

"Good Lord! There's enough money in here to buy the world. I've never seen so much in my entire life. What on earth should we do with this?"

Tom had an easy answer, "Divide it up and go home. What do you think is in there? A hundred grand? More?

"Many, many times more. Millions I'd bet."

"Unbelievable! We're rich."

I wish it was that easy, but for some reason I found that answer too simple. Many questions flooded my mind simultaneously. *Who knows we have it? Who else is looking for it and is willing to blow holes in us to get it? What's the legal thing to do with it?*

Tom was certain his idea was the best, "I'll tell you one thing for sure. You turn it in anywhere in Mexico, and it'll wind up right back in the hands of the drug gangs. Turn it in back in the States and whoever you hand it to will retire the next day. Who you gonna trust with millions?"

"You're probably right. But for the time being, let's keep this to ourselves. No need to invite trouble. It's funny, though. Bones said the gold was cursed and everybody who went after it died. He was lying about the Mayan gold, but it sure seems as if the curse was real. Everybody who has touched this bag has wound up dead. Nathan, Bones, who knows how many? I don't want my name added to the list."

"Me neither."

I zipped the bag back together and took one last glance back at the lagoon where Bones had just met his end. I couldn't help but think to myself that Bones had never discovered what was truly valuable. He had lived for only one reason for many years and when he got within reach of his goal, it had disappeared from his grasp. All the time, he was living on a beautiful old sailboat in the Keys, not understanding the value of what he already had. I vowed right then and there never to take such a misguided path.

We walked down the beach to meet Tuna and the fabled drug lord El Dorado. With his hands behind his head and his clothes soaking wet and covered in mud, he didn't have nearly the imperial look he had worked diligently to cultivate. I took the rope from the gym bag and used my best nautical knots to make certain that El Dorado would not be able to give us any more trouble. It was interesting to see how small and insignificant he really was. He was a disgusting little man who had ruined the lives of many people. When Triste saw him, he used what had to be the very last of his energy to kick El Dorado in the groin as hard as he could. El Dorado crumpled to the ground and wailed in pain.

"You're not going to let this punk torture me, are you? You're not criminals, are you?"

"You executed his father and sent his mother to work in one of your whore houses. You think we should have sympathy for scum like you? It's all I can do to keep from giving him the gun and letting him finish you right here. And trust me, you're about to pay the price for your crimes and you've got a lot to answer for. Keep moving or we'll all start kicking you."

I looked over at Tom. We were soaking wet and there was still a persistent rain falling. We looked like survivors of the Bataan Death March. "We've got to get back to the Susanne and Karen. If this creep has hurt them, I want him myself."

The conversation was not wasted on El Dorado. "I'm sure my men have them. When they see you holding me they'll know what to do. Perhaps it's time to talk a deal. You could leave here with your lives and perhaps with some of my money that thief and assassin Bones put in that bag you are holding."

"We'll decide what to do with you shortly. And I wouldn't underestimate our lady friends. If I'm not mistaken, you and your collection of idiots haven't been able to hang onto them up to this point. So just shut up and keep walking."

* * *

David and Kevin left the girls on board *Dark Lady* with Ted and Brownie while they used the cover of darkness to approach El Dorado's yacht *Diablo*. The yacht was large enough to have a boarding platform and ladder. The sole occupant was the captain.

With the wind blowing and the rain still coming down, he had elected to stay in the yacht's bridge. This limited the captain's view of anyone approaching as they climbed the steps to deck level. With his crisp, white uniform and gold epaulets adorning his slight frame, his dark hair slicked-back and a David Niven mustache, he looked more like an escapee from a 1940s B flick than captain of a fancy yacht. Of course, the holstered stainless steel .45 caliber revolver on his belt conveyed another side to his persona much more in keeping with his position. As David entered from the port side of the bridge, the Mexican immediately started to draw his gun. He was more than surprised when Kevin came up from the opposite side with a gun already in his hand. They had the proverbial drop on the captain.

"Let go of the pistol. I'm very nervous holding this gun. Ever since 'Nam, I've had nightmares about getting upset and shooting some innocent person. I'm sure you don't want that person to be you. Do you?"

"No, señor. I'm dropping it. See? It's dropped."

David picked up the captain's pistol and tucked it into his own belt. He laughed when he realized the siege of *Diablo* was over and over very quickly. "This has to be the easiest takeover of a vessel on record. You apparently don't believe in going down with the ship. Pretty smart, I'd say."

The captain was verbally defiant. "*Diablo* belongs to a very powerful man. This will mean your death when he finds out what you have done."

Kevin was a man of few words, "Bite me, greaser. Shut up and sit down."

He pushed the captain into the pilot's seat and began using a roll of conveniently-placed duct tape to make certain he wouldn't move or talk. "What now, Kevin?"

"I don't know about you, but I'm having a really good time. It's like being back in combat. Maybe I shoulda stayed in. I mean I'm getting old, fat, and lazy hauling tourists around. I need some action."

"Let's hope this is all the action you're going to see tonight. I'm concerned about the guys on shore. Jim and Tom aren't exactly warriors. We need to get ready in case El Dorado returns with his thugs. We can set up some sort of surprise for them and maybe catch them off guard. What do you think?"

"It may be a little too late for that."

"How so?"

"I hear an outboard heading our way."

"That's got to be El Dorado's speedboat. They're headed toward *Dark Lady*."

* * *

We pulled alongside the schooner. We felt we were holding an ace with El Dorado tightly bound in the bottom. We were more than relieved when Susanne came over to the rail and broke into a huge smile as she realized we were driving the boat. "We're all safe. Thank God you are. Who is that?

"Allow me to present the great El Dorado."

"Where's Bones?"

"He's not with us anymore."

"Why not?"

"He didn't make it. It's a long story. I'll tell you after we get all these creeps under control."

We gathered El Dorado and all of his men in the main salon. Even though they were tightly bound and we held all the guns, I was still very concerned about having such a collection of cutthroats near any of us. Tuna took El Dorado's power launch and headed to the yacht to check on David and Kevin. Within the hour, everyone was on *Dark Lady*.

"What do we do with these guys? We turn them into the Mexican authorities and they'll be back on the streets in an hour and be very pissed at us. The way things are in the States, I'd never feel safe. They operate about as freely there as they do in Mexico."

Always ready with a little spot of humor, David responded to that assertion. "Yes, and these guys don't look like they could landscape anything."

Tuna had been studying the situation carefully and came up with a solution that we all thought had a lot of potential. "Do you think we could get El Dopo's boat out of the lagoon in the dark?"

"I don't know why not. It's probably got GPS and we can hit the retrace route function and follow the same path it came in on to get out. Hell, just set the course and use the auto pilot."

"You're right. I don't want these guys on *Dark Lady* with us for even the rest of tonight. In my book, we're in danger as long as they're here and I'm not up to shooting anybody and throwing them overboard. Let's take them all back to their own boat. I've got the perfect answer to this."

It took two trips from *Dark Lady* to get all of the Mexicans back on their own boat. We placed them on the floor, sitting in a line inside the bridge. Only the captain remained seated in the pilot's seat. Being very concerned they might find a way to untie their bonds, we not only double and triple tied them, but duct taped their mouths and all of the knots as well. Houdini couldn't have gotten them free. As I got ready to place a nice, wide strip of tape over El Dorado's mouth, he fumed at us. "You will all die. I promise you. You don't have the cajones to kill us. Unlike you gringos, we aren't too frightened to take care of you."

I'd had enough of his rant, so I explained to him what we had in mind after I sealed his mouth tightly. "Our friend Tuna had a really great idea how to handle you. We are taking you and your boat out to open water, setting a direct course on your autopilot and then letting your beautiful yacht do the rest."

Tuna came up from the engine room. "I found what this boat must run on."

"Not diesel fuel?"

"Apparently not. The engine room has a very large supply of heroin and a weapons storage area you'd have to see to believe. Check out this silver plated .357 Smith & Wesson." Tuna had his new pistol tucked under his belt, and we were all beginning to look like a band of guerrillas with all the commandeered weapons.

"What should we do with the drugs and guns?"

"I think leaving them onboard will reinforce our plans. I've set the course on the autopilot. We throw it in gear, give the throttle a little push, and they'll be on their way."

"I have to hand it to you, Tuna. This is a stroke of genius."

"No problem. Do you want the honors or shall I?"

"It's your plan. You handle it."

Tuna grabbed the microphone on the single sideband radio. After adjusting the frequency, he finally found his target. "Yes, Miami operator? Please put me through to the United States Coast Guard. This is an emergency."

"Yes, sir. One moment please."

"This is United States Coast Guard, Key West. What's the nature of your emergency?"

"Yes, sir. We are on the yacht, *Diablo*. This is a Mexican yacht. We are Americans and have taken control of this vessel. We have prisoners on board: A Mexican drug lord and five of his men. They are all bound and unable to operate the vessel. We have set the autopilot on a course that will take the *Diablo* straight to the Dry Tortugas. It's leaving the Turneffe Islands of Belize at eight knots and there's no one at the wheel. Also, it's full of drugs and guns. I suggest you intercept immediately."

"Sir, can you give me your name? I have to ask you some questions."

"Let me ask you a question first, young man."

"Yes, sir?"

"Did you copy all of what I said?"

"Yes, sir."

"That's great. If you don't want this two hundred foot yacht running into an oil rig or a cruise ship, I suggest you get a crew onto a chopper and chase this thing down, pronto. I'll make it easy for you. We'll set off the Epirb satellite alarm, as well. You'll have no problem finding it. I'd bring six sets of handcuffs for El Dorado and crew. Look him up. Your boss will be thrilled. This is *Diablo* signing off."

"But, sir, sir? I have questions for you, sir."

Tuna shut off the radio. As soon as *Diablo* was clear of the channel, he engaged the autopilot and pushed the throttle forward. The last thing Tuna did as we headed back to the launch was to set off the Epirb unit. The Coast Guard would be on top of *Diablo* within two hours. He looked over at a dismayed El Dorado as he left the bridge.

"Been nice working with you. Have fun with the U.S. authorities."

The last thing we saw was the white stern light of *Diablo* as she steamed toward the open waters of the Gulf of Mexico and on a course that would take it straight to the Tortugas.

Before we got the high-powered launch back to *Dark Lady*, a Coast Guard Search and Rescue C-130 was already in the air headed to the source of the satellite alarm. The opportunity to intercept a major drug shipment turned the Coasties on, and they would waste no time taking home their prize. El Dorado would finish out his career in a federal prison.

As we boarded *Dark Lady*, Susanne and Karen were waiting for Tom and me with outstretched arms. Throwing myself at her was the best feeling I'd had in years. I knew there was something very special between us. Karen and Tom seemed to share that sentiment. Kevin, Ted, and Brownie insisted they needed to fly back to the mainland, even though it was very late. They hadn't taken the time to let anyone know where they were going, and they were concerned about the folks they left behind putting out an all-points bulletin. We thanked them profusely for their invaluable help and exchanged numbers so we could all get together somewhere down the road. David took them back over to the plane. As they boarded, he gave Kevin a bear hug.

"Kevin, without you guys, there's no telling what would have happened out here. You are heroes in my book." Looking every bit the part of the Red Baron, Kevin stood on the float of the plane smiling largely. He gave a big wave from the cockpit and in seconds, the little plane was on its thirty-mile flight back to the mainland. David determined he would not let such great friends disappear from his life. He'd get back up with them after things got back to normal, if that was even possible.

Though we were exhausted, we were far too exhilarated to go to sleep. We gathered in the main salon with the exception of Triste. Susanne and Karen had fixed him some hot chocolate and tucked him in. He pretended he was fine and didn't need the attention, though we all knew he appreciated it. We were down to just our crew minus Bones. Susanne pressed me for the details of what happened to him. I knew it was the best time to describe what had happened with Triste asleep in his bunk. I really didn't want to disillusion Triste about Bones. He held a deep affection for the old captain, and there wasn't any point in changing that.

"Tom and I discovered some very disturbing things about Bones. He was not even close to being the eccentric, harmless captain we all thought he was. He was the other end of the spectrum. He had been directly involved with El Dorado for most of his life. Believe it or not, the little guy was the 'heavy' for them."

Susanne, confused by the word "heavy" asked, "What does that mean? Did he transport them?"

"No. When somebody didn't do what they wanted, Bones would make them disappear. El Dorado said he even killed Nathan Hibbs who, in reality, was El Dorado's partner in the States. Nathan had hidden the money here to squirrel it away from El Dorado. Only he and Bones knew where it was. El Dorado believes Bones did away with Nathan so he had been watching him for years, waiting for Bones to make his move to grab the money."

"How much money was it? Do you have any idea what he did with it?"

"Tom and I know exactly what he did with it." I reached for the gym bag, opened it up in front of the group and dumped it all on the table. The amount was even more staggering than I had thought.

"Take a look for yourselves. Bones died trying to claim it. Anybody got any suggestions as to what we should do with it? The way I see it, we are all in this equally. Who thinks we should turn it in to the authorities?"

David had the right answer to that question. "Uh, which branch of government is the most honest? I'd hate to turn over millions of dollars to a couple of cash-starved government types. To tell you the truth, I don't see a lot of difference between the greed of El Dorado and the greed of our government. I say we just split it up and keep quiet about it."

In my opinion, Tom had the best idea of all: "My thought is that we put the money back into the bag, get out a bottle of Bones' rum, and try to forget what a hell of a day we've had."

Tom's suggestion was seconded by everyone, so Tuna quickly scored a bottle from the captain's quarters. We passed the bottle around the salon table.

"To the old scoundrel, Captain Bones. Never was there a more despicable, black hearted pirate than he, and without whom none of us would be together this evening. And let's not forget a toast to adventure and new loves."

The table gave a chorus of cheers and we downed what would become the first of a half dozen or so tribute shots.

In looking back over the day's events, we all realized just how lucky we were to be alive. Certainly, most of the people who had ever had a run-in with El Dorado had not fared so well. It was now after midnight, the rum had taken the edge off our adrenalin rush, and our eyelids were starting to fall shut of their own accord.

Tomorrow would be a day for very big decisions. We were a long way from home on a boat with no captain, a couple of lovely women, and a gym bag full of money. The Coast Guard would undoubtedly be looking for us, as they would have already been aboard *Diablo* and learned who tied up El Dorado and crew. In addition, there were two bodies somewhere in the lagoon that would need to be explained, if the sharks had left anything to find. Tomorrow would be a full day.

I looked over at Susanne and she nodded, indicating it was time to turn in. We saw the same signal between Tom and Karen. How interesting that we came down here for a relaxing vacation and wound up not only with the most extraordinary experience of our lives, but also in the company of two wonderful women. As tired as we were, Susanne and I still found the energy to avail ourselves of each other's charms before we collapsed into a deep, sound slumber. As we slept, the rain that had accompanied us the entire day was still falling ever so lightly and the rhythmic sounds of the drops played a percussion solo over our heads on deck. Other than the rain's gentle refrain, all was quiet.

Later that night, a light wind started to fill in. I could usually detect any change in conditions by the noise a ship's rigging made as it rattled against the rails and spars. It wasn't a strong wind, but enough to add a little rattling to the night's music. Suddenly, a new and noticeably different sound came from the main salon. At first I assumed that another crewmember awoke to use the head or get a glass of water but the noise sounded 'off' somehow, and loud enough to cause me to stir and wake Susanne.

"What's that, Jim?"

"Somebody's up."

"Should we check it out? I'll go with you."

I admired her courage and fire. There wasn't much she was afraid of. We got out of our bunk and quickly dressed. I pulled on my jeans; Susanne threw on my shirt, which covered her almost as fully as a nightgown, and we walked together down the hall to the salon. Instead of finding the overhead lights on, we were surprised to see a small beam of light from a flashlight circling the room. Since all of our cabins had doors, there was no reason not to cut on the salon light. I walked over to the switch and flipped on the cabin's light. The person standing in front of us almost made my legs give out.

"Bones! I thought you were dead. I saw the shark pull you under. How did you get yourself out of that?"

"Hawkins, my good friend, Old Bones ain't all that easy to kill. If I were, I'd have been gone years ago. It was a huge hammerhead all right. Almost twelve feet long, I'd say. When he came for me I let him taste a little bit of me and he didn't much like plastic and steel." Bones reached over and tapped his prosthetic leg. "You could say I gave him the boot."

"You tried to give Tom and me the boot, as well. We're still alive, no thanks to you."

"Hawkins. It seems I have more confidence in you and Tom than you do yourself. I knew exactly what you'd do. You figured it out and here you are. No worse for wear."

"Why are you here? The Coast Guard has El Dorado by now and they'll be here to talk with us any minute. I'm sure you don't want to have an interview with any form of government."

"You're right about that. As much as I'm going to miss you all, I have to leave and I'll be taking my money with me, if you will be so kind as to show me where the bag is."

As he spoke, Bones made no secret of the pistol he held by his side. We had seen his ability to use one earlier in the day and had no doubt he would do whatever he needed to do to get his hands on the money. We heard footsteps as Tom, Tuna, and David came into the salon. They were as surprised as we had been.

Never at a loss for words, Bones greeted them, "Good evening, crew. Your captain has returned. I can't stay and steer *Dark Lady* home, however. I think you're all perfectly capable of that by now. I just came to get what's mine and wish you all the best. How is my young friend Triste?"

"He's in his cabin. We didn't tell him about your true nature." I reached into the locker where we had thrown the bag, grabbed it, and tossed it toward Bones' feet. "Here's your bag."

"You'll forgive me, Hawkins, if I appear to not trust you folks, but I've got a lot of time invested in this enterprise, and I need to make sure no one has been playing around with my prize."

Bones reached deep into the bag and determined his ill-gotten gains were all still there. In a surprise gesture, he pulled a large stack of bills from the bag and dropped them on the salon table.

"Hawkins, here's what I want you to do with this. You see that young Triste goes to the States and gets a good education. Not just a good one, the best money can buy. And you fellas help him rebury his old man, and if his mother is still alive, you bring her to live with him. He's a good kid and deserves a lot better than he's gotten. I don't want him ending up like me."

He reached back down in the bag and grabbed another large stack of bills.

"This is to take care of *Dark Lady*. I may never get to see her again, but she's been good to me and I don't want her rotting in some Godforsaken harbor. You fellas can have her, but I want her taken care of. You all okay with this?"

"You're holding the gun, Bones. We'll see that Triste gets what you asked. We would have done that anyway, but the money will help."

"That's good. I've got to get going now but I just want to say that you have been the best bunch I ever sailed with. I'd trust you with anything. I don't say that too many folks, so you can consider it a compliment. Well, I'm outta here. Don't come topside for fifteen minutes. Don't make me have to be a bad guy. Got it?"

"We got it."

"Good evening to you all. And Miss Susanne, don't let go of him. You've got a good one there."

Susanne grabbed my arm and looked at me. "I know, Bones."

In less than a minute, Bones had gone topsides, lowered himself into El Dorado's high-powered launch and was gone. We could hear the whine of the motor until it was out of range. We never figured out where he went or how he made good his escape. Of all the people I'd ever met, he had to be the most unusual character. In the end, he had shown a spark of decency, so perhaps his time with us on *Dark Lady* had helped him turn his life around. I guess we'll never know.

13

Diablo sped along through the ocean at ten knots making a straight course for Florida with the help of the auto pilot and a high-dollar global positioning satellite receiver. Tuna had also had the forethought to start the running lights and even a deck light so that the yacht would be very visible at night. Diablo's captain was seated in the overstuffed chair in the bridge with a bird's eye view of the sea. To say he was highly nervous would be a colossal understatement. He knew the numbers of fishing boats, tugs, oil rigs and cruise ships that plied those waters, and he was terrified they would steam into one of them and all drown while he was tied tightly to his chair.

El Dorado and all of his men, including the captain, had their mouths taped shut. Tuna surmised they might attempt to chew off each other's ropes if they could get their mouths close to them. This fact made it very difficult for the captain to scream when he first spotted the huge ocean liner directly ahead. He strained to gauge the distance and path of *Diablo* against the mammoth liner, and could almost guarantee they were on a direct collision course. With only a mile or so to go to impact, he saw a huge spotlight from above light up the front of *Diablo.* Soon he heard the undulating sound of a military helicopter as it hovered above them.

It was not a cruise liner. It was a very large Coast Guard frigate that routinely patrolled the Gulf of Mexico. The ship's main focus was drug interdiction and this was going to be a huge catch for them. Lines appeared on the lighted decks from above and in short order soldiers wearing black uniforms swarmed the deck. The captain of *Diablo* continued to watch, terrified, as the frigate suddenly turned a swift twenty degrees to avoid the collision. Never before had a collection of killers and thugs been so happy to see the authorities. They were alive for the time being, but they were now in the custody of the United States Coast Guard and any attempts at bribery and collusion would surely fail. Federal prisons awaited them all.

* * *

It didn't take the Coast Guard long to find us. By breakfast the next morning, there was a very large cutter tied alongside *Dark Lady*. It was a pretty intimidating experience having that sleek vessel with its deck-mounted, fifty-caliber machine gun come alongside. They were certainly business-like as they boarded. They were young and aggressive. To say they were a little incredulous after meeting us to discover we had gotten the best of El Dorado and put them on a course to rendezvous with the Coast Guard would be an understatement. The captain of the cutter was a young man named Joe Thurber. He was about forty-five years old and senior to most of his crew by twenty years. He had a prepared set of questions that the U.S. government wanted answered. We each told them the same exact story, just as it had unfolded. The most telling moment was when they got Triste off to the side and he corroborated everything we had said even before they interviewed him. The young radiate innocence. By the time they were finished questioning him, they felt they had gotten the truth.

"Who's going to be the captain of the *Dark Lady* on your return to the States?"

The crew looked at me and even though they were all equally capable, I was proud to be their choice. "I guess it's me, Captain Thurber."

"Fine. You understand that the Justice Department will undoubtedly need to interview you all over the course of the investigation and for El Dorado's trial?"

"We'll be there when you need us. Count on it."

With that, they left us. We were back down to our original group, plus Susanne, Karen and Triste. There was some concern over the cash Bones had left, but we had all agreed and that information was not volunteered to the authorities.

We determined that sailing back to either Belize or Mexico would not be wise, so we motored *Dark Lady* around Ambergris Caye to the developed side of the island to take on fuel and supplies for our trip back to Florida.

Ambergris was spectacular with white sand beaches and lush vegetation. Even though our plan was to leave as soon as we had taken on supplies, the presence of a small, thatched-roof cantina made us rethink our departure plans. We were still worn out and felt one more night in paradise wouldn't affect anyone's plans.

We spent the morning cleaning up *Dark Lady* and preparing for the long sail home. At lunch we visited a great restaurant, and I bought the first round of beer for the crew. We had lived through some pretty remarkable events over the past couple of weeks, which made it very difficult to embellish our recounting of the experience. We were sailors, however, so we were working on that issue as hard as we could. We found our way to the small cantina around four in the afternoon and were delighted to see a three-piece reggae band setting up their equipment. Since we had already put down quite a few beers, the band sounded every bit as good as Bob Marley. We sang along with the songs, bought drinks for the band, and danced the night away.

As I sat back enjoying the evening in the very small, unpretentious cantina, I realized that there's really nothing more important in life than love and friendship. I never believed in love at first sight prior to meeting Susanne, but she had changed my outlook on many things in a very short period of time. As I watched her standing by the bandstand and swaying sensually to the beat, I felt anxious to learn every small detail that made her who she was. Susanne and Karen had both elected to return to Florida with us and I hoped I could persuade her, by the time we arrived, to move in with me. I thought she would be receptive but I'd wait until closer to home to broach the subject.

The next morning we were ready to get underway shortly after dawn. We had received a little burst of good-news-bad-news at the marina where we fueled up. Since I was already late getting back to work and needed at least another week to make the trip, one call home and my boss informed me that my services were no longer needed. Susanne said that sometimes God takes actions on one's behalf when one is either unable or unwilling to do so, and that this was one of those times. After thinking about it a bit, I had to agree with her. I did feel a load lift from my shoulders when he told me to not rush back. Since Tom and David were self-employed they didn't have my problem. Tuna had a job, but he was the boss, so he needn't worry. Susanne and Karen were both teachers, and I didn't know how long they had off and didn't want to remind them of it. I wanted her stay with me rather than go home anyway. I gathered that Tom felt the same way about Karen. David had decided to not make the return trip with us. He was still in a hurry to get home and try to get back together with his wife.

Originally, he was going to retrace his journey on the ferry, but then had second thoughts about interfacing with so many strangers. We had all had enough adventure to last a long time. His alternate plan worked out nicely.

We watched as the old seaplane circled the harbor and then glided to a smooth landing. The plane taxied over to where David was waiting on shore. He threw his bag aboard after we all wished him well. Kevin sat smiling in the cockpit. Within moments, they were airborne and out of sight. David said he'd check in with us when we got to Florida and let us know how it all worked out.

At best, it was a week's sail. None of us were in a hurry to get back, and I was determined to savor every moment with Susanne. This was as close to living out my fantasies as I'd ever had, or ever would have. We finally untied our lines and headed out the channel.

As if Mother Nature was suddenly on our side, we received a favorable breeze out of the west. If the wind direction held, we could run a tight reach north and then a broad reach toward the coast of Florida. The sun came out warm in the afternoon and we were all in shorts and tee shirts enjoying a brisk sail back home.

Dark Lady was art in motion. We marveled at how well she sailed and how wonderful it felt to share the ocean with her. She was nautical royalty and we had been privileged enough to share this voyage on her.

That evening Susanne and I took the watch from ten to midnight. The moon came out almost full and lit the sky and ocean so we could see for miles, and it was warm and spectacular. I held her close beside me and knew full well she understood my feelings for her. She made no secret of the fact that she felt the same. We didn't know what the future held for us, but we did know it would be together.

Throughout the next five days, our crew enjoyed the trip we had thought we would be on all along. The events of the previous weeks seemed but distant memories. The weather remained beautiful, and each day was lovelier than the previous one. Dolphins played in our bow wave for hours at a time and at night the stars gave us an illuminated canopy fueling our desire to keep on sailing. We made one last stop at the Dry Tortugas on the way home. I had given such glowing descriptions to Susanne that she had to see the place for herself. We snorkeled in the crystal clear water and lay out on the deck of the boat for the better part of the day. We were refreshed and ready to be home and start a new chapter in our lives.

Tuna was taking Triste under his wing and said that he would be looking out for him when we got back home. He would help him locate his relatives and also get a proper burial for his father. Of course, he would be going to high school and then on to college. His life had taken a dramatic turn for the better.

As we looked back over the trip and all it had produced, Susanne shared her thoughts with me. "You know, it's funny how life works out."

"How so?"

"You all came on this trip chasing a fantasy about cruising. You fell into another man's wild chase for treasure, and the truth is that we all found our own treasure. David is heading back to his wife and kids; Tuna and Triste will both be enriched from helping one another; Tom found Karen; and I found you."

"Indeed you did. You are wise beyond your years my love."

14

We arrived back in Florida all too soon. The week had gone by like an hour. We had all chosen new courses that we would take in the days ahead. David, with Leigh and the twin boys met us at the dock. They decided to take a few days off and come down to greet us. It was easy to see they had settled some of their issues. They were full of smiles.

Jim, Susanne, Leigh and David

The entire crew got together again at the Buccaneer Bar to celebrate the end of one adventure and the beginning of several new ones. I offered the first of many toasts that would be put forth that evening. "It's hard to believe we were here to charter a sailboat just a few weeks ago, and we were all in a very different place and state of mind. A lot has happened, good and bad, but I think we're all better for the experience.

"A toast to the crew of *Dark Lady*." David held up a local paper "We are the story in the Keys. Of course, they don't know who we are, so we'll just be famous to ourselves."

The newspaper cover read, "Sailors send drug kingpin to the Keys with many keys aboard." The article told how the Coast Guard had been alerted by a mystery ship and that El Dorado and his men had been bound and gagged when they boarded. They had been taken to Miami to await prosecution. There was a lot of guessing and pondering throughout the Keys as to just who was involved, but we had all decided to keep our story to ourselves and that's what we were doing. We didn't need any friends of El Dorado coming across the border to pay us a social call.

Karen and Tom

We stayed up very late. We hated to see the day end, as our paths would be taking different directions in the morning. The bartender finally ran us out of the place around 2:00 a.m. There were a few moist eyes as we hugged and said our goodbyes. Even lifelong friends Susanne and Karen would be separating, at least for a while. Tom and Karen were buying a sailboat of their own and heading out for ports unknown. We were sure that wherever they went, there would be palm trees and clear water. Tuna and Triste shoved off for Raleigh. Susanne and I were the last two still aboard the schooner.

We decided to move to Marathon permanently to try to make a go of it taking charters on *Dark Lady*. With our share of the money Bones had left for *Dark Lady*, we could keep up the boat and live reasonably well. I also unveiled a new plan that had been on my bucket list for quite some time.

"I'm going to write a book, a novel to be precise."

"That so? What's it going to be about?"

"It's the story of four guys and how they wanted to go sailing. They wind up on a wild treasure hunt with a madman and ended up falling in love."

Susanne slid over close beside me and threw her arms around my shoulders. She looked up into my eyes and smiled that incredible smile of hers. "Wow, that's sounds exciting. A little too farfetched to be believable, but fun. Can I help you with the research?"

"I'm glad you mentioned that. I was going to ask you to help me with the love part. I'm not very experienced in those sorts of things and wanted some expert opinions."

"You got it, Captain Hawkins."

We embraced and started to get so engrossed in our "research" that we had to return to the boat to finish our studies.

Dark Lady would be available whenever our friends wanted to come down. We all owned shares in her from here on out. Susanne was right. I had not only found out who I was; I had found a treasure far greater than the one Bones had been searching for all that time.

Epilogue

The elegant bar at the Fortunary Hotel was full of well-heeled tourists and world travelers. It had a reputation among the world's elite of being one of the must-see places for many years. For decades, it had been the epicenter of South America's privileged and wealthy elites. Located in Rio de Janeiro, its turn-of-the-century elegance remained pristine with brass railings and polished marble floors. Chandeliers hung from the ceiling and the well-bred patrons in the Decatur Bar added greatly to the atmosphere and enjoyed the absolutely regal elegance that surrounded them. It was truly a place for people-watching if you wanted to get a firsthand look at the rich and famous.

In the corner of the bar was a three-piece jazz band providing background music from the likes of Duke Ellington and Henry Mancini. Several couples expertly stepped through a waltz on the polished mahogany dance floor. A number of the men wore tailored tuxedos as dinnertime required formal attire and none of them would dare visit the grand casino adjacent to the hotel in anything less than a tux. The women were spectacular, to say the least. Mostly middle-aged, covered in jewelry by Cartier, donning designer gowns that cost as much as automobiles, they were the arm candy of the business tycoons and well-born men who squired them about.

In the corner of the bar, at a small table sat one woman, far more beautiful than the rest. She was not only younger than most of the women there, she was striking to the point of distraction. Her looks gathered the admiration of every man in the room and the glares of all the other women. She was the proverbial Scarlet

O'Hara and she knew it. Her every movement spoke of grace, confidence, and intellect. Few men would ever be so privileged to find themselves in her adoring company. She was everything a man could hope for. It was also apparent that she was very aware of the talents she possessed and had no intention of settling for less than the best of what life had to offer. Of course, this included men.

On this particular evening, she had decided to visit the bar by herself. She enjoyed the music this band put forth and saw no need to not enjoy them even though none of her regular admirers was in town. It was about the time the band started to play a marvelous instrumental interpretation of Earl Gardner's "Misty" that he caught her eye as he entered the room. Dressed entirely in black with a red trimmed cape and wide brimmed fedora, he strode into the room and then paused to take in his surroundings. His complexion was dark and his grey Van Dyke beard framed his granite face elegantly. She had hoped she might meet him. Rumors that he was back in town had been circulating for days. To her thinking, there was nothing quite as intriguing about a man as a degree of mystery, and Arman Ropere had that in spades. A uniformed attendant came over to him.

"Sir, may I take your cloak?"

"Thank you, young man."

"Yes, sir. So good to have you back with us again. Will you require a table or do you wish to sit at the bar?"

Arman looked around the room. He was not fazed by the number of patrons looking back at him. He was a major source of curiosity to those in the room. Rumors of exactly who he was had circulated among the aristocracy for weeks since his yacht moved into the prestigious Lands' End Resort and Marina. It was a magnificent vessel, almost two hundred feet in length and staffed by a professional crew who wore white, starched uniforms. Arman caught a glimpse of the beautiful young woman, and she made no attempt to suppress her smile. He had seen that look before, and she had the style and appearance that appealed to his refined taste.

"I think I'll take a table. I'll find one myself if that's all right."

"Absolutely, sir. Anywhere you like."

Arman strode confidently over to the young woman's table. "Good evening. My name is Arman Ropere. Are you by yourself this evening?"

"I am." The young woman extended her gloved hand. "I'm Jody Augustine. I know who you are. Your reputation precedes you."

"My reputation? I was unaware that I had a reputation."

"Please, Arman. False modesty is unbecoming. You must be aware that everyone in Rio wants to know more of the dark mystery man who appeared out of the blue last year. No one seems to have a clue as to where you came from or how you made your fortune, for that matter."

"That's interesting to hear. May I join you?"

"Be my guest."

As Arman moved over to her table the maître d' immediately pulled out the chair for him. "May I take your cane, sir?"

Arman took his polished teak cane with a bronze tip and silver Cobra's head for a handle and handed it to the attendant. It was apparent as he sat that he had an issue maneuvering.

"You have a problem with your leg?"

"It's not a problem, really. I learned to live with it years ago."

"How did it happen?"

"Shark attack."

"Oh my God. You're so lucky to be alive."

"You don't know the half of it, my dear. What would you like to know about me? I'm not really a mystery."

"Where did you come from, how did you make your fortune? I'd love to hear more about your yacht."

"One of my favorite subjects, my yacht. It belonged to a friend of mine who, well, let's say, found himself unable to use it any longer. I bought it at auction, actually through a private intermediary. I always fancied it. It used to be called *Diablo* but I thought that rather depressing, so I renamed it *Triste* after a friend. And my career. Where to begin? I've actually had several. I started in the military where I handled special assignments. After that, I eased into the pharmaceutical business. You know what with all the Baby Boomers in the States, there's a lot of folks with health concerns. Most recently, I've been in the salvage business. I made most of my fortune that way. Well, my dear, now that I've enlightened you as to my sordid past, can I interest you in a drink? I'll have a rum but for you, how about a Madeira?"

photograph by Robert Dumon Photography

About the Author

Les Pendleton lives in historic New Bern, North Carolina. His writing style conveys the influence of his career in motion pictures. Many people share their impression that reading his novels feels as if you are watching the characters come to life on the silver screen. Actual locations in coastal North Carolina are featured in many of his books. His writing spans a wide array of genres from action adventure, romance, historical fiction, suspense-filled mysteries and autobiographies. Les spends every free moment with his family and friends sailing in Pamlico Sound and the Atlantic Coast.

For more about the author, visit **www.lespendleton.com**

* * *

Thank you for reading this novel.
We invite you to share your thoughts and reactions
***by going to* Amazon.com/author/lespendleton**
and posting a review.

Essie Press

Made in the USA
Monee, IL
13 September 2021